I0525196

Beneath the Veil

DAVID NOE

Amazing Things Press

Book design by Julie L. Casey
Cover art by Dærick Gröss Sr.
Interior art by Paul Tuma

This book is a work of fiction. Any names, characters, or incidents are the product of the author's imagination and are used fictitiously. Any resemblance to actual events, locales, or persons, living or dead is purely coincidental.

ISBN 978-1945667435

Printed in the United States of America.

For more information, visit

www.authordavidnoe.weebly.com
or
www.amazingthingspress.com

We often hear that the west was wild…

Yes, but there were miles upon miles of not much of anything at all, and when the folks came, when the people moved into those virgin places, they brought their secrets with them. Their long shadows followed behind them and took up residence in the grass and the scrub and the tiny towns that all too often were ghost towns…

even before they were empty.

As the new century approached, many of the old ways stayed entrenched. For that is what old ways do. That is why they are old. Veils are hung to hide the past so that outsiders will pass right on through. The future abhors those veils and eventually seeks to tear them down and gaze beneath. Men of vision light torches and pave new roads. They find the old paths and make them new.

There is ugliness beneath the veil. It churns men's stomachs and turns their hearts to stone. Still they look. Still they search. Still they uncover the layers so purposely laid and fastened and tied.

Why…?

It's because the wounds beneath the wraps need the air and the light in order to heal. It's because the beasts cannot be tamed in the dark.

We often hear the west was wild…

Now find out why.

DEDICATED TO
My grandfather
William James "Ga-Ga" Barngrover
A real cowboy

CHAPTER ONE

Three bullets this time, and it didn't look like I was going to live long enough to be a grizzled old man. One bullet came within inches of my cheek, smashing through the thin weathered outhouse wall. The second, near my shoulder, ventilated the crapper again. The third shot grazed my thigh just enough to tear it open like a frenzy of half mad fire ants.

"SSsssss…" I clamped my needle sharp teeth together and breathed all the pain in. I had to stay quiet. I only had the upper hand because they couldn't see me.

They were firing wild. They'd seen me ride into the glorified miner's camp called Pressure Hill. Even at age seventeen, I knew the land better than they did. I used the wind, the setting sun, the sounds to my advantage. I knew where they were long before they knew that I knew where they were. I had a chance to gather my gear and send New Moon off to safety before they tried the ambush.

I slipped into the shadows and had them firing at a cactus. They were disorganized at first. Their shots sounded like stones beneath a wagon wheel. Now though, they were walking the path between the few standing abandoned buildings, shooting holes through the walls in an orchestrated pattern, reloading and calmly perforating any structure that could hide the bounty hunter freak called the Alabaster Kid.

"Yer luck cain't hold out fer long, kid," Zakk Griller yelled into the darkness, hoping for a reply to target.

The good part about me sending New Moon away meant that my horse was safe. The bad part of course, meant that I

1

was trapped here. The best part however, was that the sun had set. It was a dark night, and the advantage had just swung my way.

They weren't too stupid. They had managed to rob a store in Limbley and get away from the law. They had managed to lay low for nearly a month, living off the streams and wooded areas of Northwest Missouri. There was a rumor that they had a network of helpers, family members, cousins throughout the area that helped them with their crimes. The weather had been on their side too, with low rains and decent temperatures. Even now they stood back to back to back with no light to give away their position. Their guns were fully loaded. They were ready and listening. I had them right where I wanted them.

I made the call of a chattering raccoon to cover my footfalls. They tensed and pointed their weapons but quickly realized it was just a raccoon stirred up from the ruckus. I now stood fully revealed in the alley, enveloped only by the night. They could look right at me and see only shadow in the dark. What sane man would come out from hiding while three guns sought to end his life?

My advantage was that I could see them perfectly. These eyes that were so sensitive to the sun could find a blade of grass in the dark with almost no light source around. An overcast moonless night like this even hid the occasional bluish glow my strange eyes reflected. I was invisible.

They stepped and fired as one into an old wall. Then they repositioned. I took the opportunity of the noise to ready my Colt and fire at the leg of Tommy Griller. Even as he fell, the others fired at me. I leapt left behind a roof support on a wooden walkway. My leg burned in pain but not nearly as bad as Tommy's leg. He was rolling on the ground wailing. His firearm was several feet away from him.

Even though he couldn't see me, Zakk Griller ran right at me. Lenny Fish ducked down to the ground. Right as the large barrel of a man got to me, I grabbed his head and knocked him into the old pillar so hard that the beam pulled loose of the roof. The whole thing collapsed on top of him as I jumped away right towards the gun of Lenny Fish.

I could see in a flurry of slowed time what Fish could not, and most assuredly what Tommy Griller could not. As the roof collapsed, Tommy found his gun and fired in my direction just as Fish raised his own gun to my head. Tommy fired wild and first and he hit Fish in the neck. Lenny Fish fired wild too as he fell to the ground dead, before I even landed on top of him. I rolled in the dusty road, jumped up, and kicked the gun from Tommy Griller's shaking hand. Then I knocked the consciousness from him with the heel of my boot.

The Griller gang lay defeated at my feet. I just needed to patch up the two living ones and hope I could get them to Saint Joe before they died. I could then hunt down their stash and bring it back. Then came the hardest part of all, collecting my bounty. It was going to be a long night.

CHAPTER TWO

Some time after the war in Heaven when angels fought angels, but some time before the fall of man, there were demons upon the earth. These misshapen monstrosities were the casualties of war, creatures who now feared the light, beasts from both sides. They were much like the survivors of our nation's last great war, the War Between the States, the war that set out to determine whether the individual should govern himself or if the State should decree. These demons were in anguish. They were in a world that no longer accepted them, one that would lance them like a boil. They only wished to crawl into the shadows and hide away in the dark thickets among the other thorns. They gnashed at themselves and attacked any who came near. At all times, they were both running from the anguish and seeking the pain, anything to feel again, anything that might show what was real and what was a lie, black from white, day from night in a world of gray and blue and red. They were banished to the spirit realm and endless limbo once man was cast from Eden, but their likeness lived on in the hearts of sinful mankind.

They still seek release. They still claw at the roots, trying to dig themselves out of the mire, praying for some sort of redemption or release, yet fearing the light necessary for the cleansing. They cry for truth while fearing the knowledge it brings.

I know this to be fact or I have faith that it is so. I don't have the Word to lead me on this. I have but myself and the stories that speak to my core. The wisdom of my years extends beyond them. My mother knew this. She, a Bible-fed believer, knew there was more to me than my age. There simply had to be. Why would God create such a mockery of a human without just cause? Why would He allow that baby to be found in a rotting cabin, surrounded by death, if He didn't have a plan?

The answer could be two-fold, but my adopted family never spoke it. God indeed could have created this human being to do special things. It could also be that this being He created was not human in the least. There have also been times, I must confess, when I have doubts. I wonder if God was the one who created me at all.

It seems I have special insight into the hearts of men. It's merely speculation, really, or over-inflated hubris. Perhaps I just always see the worst in people. They often deliver it in spades.

It has been a little over a year now since I earned my *nom de guerre*. It was an experience that, I am ashamed to say, reminded me at the time of the stations of the cross. It seems that even I, who should know better, have that human pride which seeks to elevate or equate himself with the Divine. Nevertheless, the crowd that gathered to see my torn flesh likened it to alabaster. But alabaster doesn't bleed. Alabaster can take a whip. Alabaster doesn't seek out revenge and call it justice. In any case, I was branded the Alabaster Kid.

I took that mockery as my own. I became a new man after that event nearly a year ago, although I can still scarcely bring myself to speak of it. It seemed a lifetime ago, and it was a rebirth of sorts, one of many that made me wonder how many rebirths a man is allowed. How many times can a man approach Death and walk away anew?

In a way, it was never really death I feared. I was alive with death. It was my companion. I had seen more death than many my age, barring those soldiers now over thirty-three years past. It seems I brought my own wars with me wherever

I went. It seems I was awash in it. It seems the entire century had been.

In just a couple of years, this century would be over. A new dawn awaited, a new beginning, a rebirth for us all. There was much talk of it already as if we had to wait to be born again, as if we had a sentence to live out. There was much talk of the new, but I knew that this twentieth century would be just as full of darkness and death as any other. Man had picked away at the scab of original sin, that bleeding scar of decay that infected each individual. Man had tried many methods to purge the plague, but usually only succeeded in opening the wound, spilling even more blood on the land that God created.

While wandering in the wilderness, searching for my true calling, I was brought to the realization that my gifts were best used to bat away those shades intent on spreading evil. I was bathed in a trial of fire and realized that if I were indeed human, then I had that human weakness of choice. I would fight for the light even if the light wanted naught to do with me. I would gird myself with rags, hide myself away from the sun in order to track the villains through the fire and through their very ranks. They would know that even if it were possible to flaunt the laws of man, the laws of God had a protector.

New Moon gave up a low grunt like he was clearing his throat. It was a nudge, along with the shiver of his mane, to break me free of my night mind and alert me to a change in the environment. Immediately I noticed it too. I tended to ride off trail to avoid being seen, following closely but out of sight. The night air carried the smell of a campfire over the bluff where the trail was open and a campfire would not be wise. A Kansas bluff isn't really much of one, and if you guess that what you will find on the other side is pretty much what you were seeing on the side you were already on, then you called that bluff perfectly. There were some parts of the state though, around the edges, where the hills actually existed and the gullies sometimes washed. With my night vision, it wasn't difficult to see the light even before I topped the hill. It was like a dancing glow washing up and down over the scrub and dying October grass yet below the stars, and always out of reach.

The trail here followed an old riverbed. The Indians had used it for hundreds of years, but there weren't many Indians left in these parts, especially not out and wandering the countryside at night. I pulled my well-worn strips of cloth out of my side bag and wrapped my face. It was a practice I had long since become expert in. On the farm, it was primarily to protect me from the sun. I burned quickly and deeply when it baked my flesh. Later I learned that the fear and suspicion of men could sear like any cloudless August blast. Panic led to rash actions. The rags soothed the panic. Let their imaginations fill in my face. It was better than the truth. I could just tell them I was burned in a fire. It was true enough. In minutes I had laced the main strip around my head, tying and twisting it in the back, flattening it in the front around my eyes in a way that didn't obstruct my vision, around my mouth in a manner that allowed for movement but still remained in place, and under the bottom of my nose to let me breathe easily and pick up scents that most people couldn't.

Finally, I pulled my fillet knife out from under a hidden slit in my saddle. The knife had been a gift from a man who took me in after my unbidden orphan state when I was twelve. He was the town butcher and he taught me everything about the bodies of dead animals. He was also the town undertaker. I learned a lot there as well. I slid the thin knife down the wraps at the back of my neck, resting the cold agile blade against my skin, turning it with the crook of my neck, tucking the naked handle under the flap at the base of my skull. Having others not know what was under these wraps kept me safe in more ways than one. In my line of work, there were times when firearms were inappropriate and fists were insufficient.

I topped the hill on foot. I left New Moon untethered behind me. I wanted to arrive unobserved. Through luck most probably, the driver of the double wagons had positioned himself directly behind the campfire. My direct line of sight was blocked. The light muted my night sight, and the cackling dancing flames played havoc with my sense of smell.

Near as I could see, he had no idea I was approaching, even as I stood on the periphery of the circle of light. He was eating. His rifle was a good three feet away and was leaning on an open box of tools. From what I could tell, he was a fairly lean man, just a few years older than me. He wasn't from around here. His hat and boots were new, and the stitching on his black vest was too decorative. He had a fancy black tie and shiny blue buttons on his shirtsleeves. He was also more clean-shaven than the farmers and ranchers in this part of the country.

His double hitched wagon had a problem with an axle from the looks of it, and his horses seemed uneasy, stepping up and down, raising their head and sniffing at the air. I pulled out my Colt and stepped into the light.

"Good Lord!" He dropped his plate and lunged for his gun. "Who the blazes are you?"

"Stay right there!" I froze him with my command.

"Look, I…" he raised his hands and sat back up on his rock, "I'm just a delivery man. I'm heading up to Veil with a load of glass. I don't have…"

"Stifle yourself!"

"Is it money you want?" He lowered one hand. "I just have a few dollars is all… here in my wallet."

"I said…" I pulled out my other Colt and tried to look around the fire, "shut up!"

He dove for his gun. I shot twice. That was all that was necessary.

CHAPTER THREE

"YEEE-AAAH!" a scream erupted from between the wagons.

Harris Ferrell fell from the shadows. His gun dropped, along with a portion of his hand that he wouldn't be using again. I holstered both Colts and ran at the fire. I leapt up and over and right next to the stunned well-dressed man near the rock. One more leap and I was atop Harris Ferrell. He was writhing in pain and rolling on the ground, holding his damaged hand. He was seemingly oblivious to the fact that I was on top of him, holding him down. I, on the other hand, was keenly aware of my surroundings. The rush of the action raised my senses, my strength, and speed to their peak. It seemed I could fairly see the night wind itself, like I could smell the dirt and the blood and the creatures beyond the campsite, like the world turned slowly all around me. Ferrell screamed into unconsciousness. It was just as well. I knelt down on the wrist of his shattered hand to keep him from bleeding out. A quick glance behind my right shoulder let me know that the glass deliveryman had found his rifle and was standing cautiously beside the fire.

"What's going on here?" he demanded in a voice that wasn't so sure it was ready to speak.

"I just saved your life and now I'm attempting to save his." I took my hat off and set it on the ground. "I must stop him from losing too much blood. He has some answers for me."

"You just shot that man!" The glass man took a step towards us. "Are you... Who are you?"

A low warning rattle came from deep in my throat. I hated it. I had no control over it. It was something that had started about five years ago, right after the...

"... fire!" The glass man had been talking to no one who was listening, but now backed up a few steps at the odd sound rising up from my throat. "You just leapt right over it!"

I turned my attention to Harris Ferrell. With New Moon over the ridge, my only access to a tie-off was the one I was wearing over my face. I sneered at the necessity. I slipped the knife from the rags at the base of my neck and cut the knot at the top of my head. That one tie kept the entire mask in place. Loosening it enabled me to unravel it all. Folding it in half and again, I wrapped it tightly around Ferrell's wrist until the blood slowed and stopped. His pallor had already lightened. I would need to get him to town before dawn. The jailhouse would have the liquids he needed to help him survive.

"I know who you are..." the glass man nearly whispered. I could feel his gaze as he examined the back of my bald head, my large pointed ears, and my bluish-white skin. "You're that demon bounty hunter they're calling the Alabaster Kid. They're talking about you clear up north. I figured you were a myth to scare highwaymen. I never figured..."

"You make a real target standing there by the fire." I tied off the bandages and cut the loose ends. "Standing directly in the light reveals you."

He put his free hand under his vest where he hid his pistol. Then he backed up a step or two into the edge of the darkness. I picked up my hat with one hand and Ferrell with the other. I flung him over my shoulder with ease. We were both covered in blood and dust and dew, him more so than I.

"They say you have the strength of ten men." The glass man clutched his rifle tightly and kept his other hand firmly on his pistol.

"Is that what they say?" I couldn't help but smile. He didn't have to know that my burst of strength was only during times of intense struggle and would soon be fleeting, leaving me temporarily exhausted.

I hung my head as I turned to him and shifted my weight so that the shadow of Ferrell's body cast across my face. I placed my hat on my head at an angle to further darken my visage. I knew from experience that the fire would pick up and flicker in the white of my sharp teeth and the reflection of my eyes. There were times this had a desired effect but not this time.

"I'll be borrowing one of your horses." I laid Ferrell over the back of the closest beast. It whinnied softly in response. I placed my hand on its neck and 'spoke' back to it in the same dulcet tones, nearly imperceptibly.

"Don't worry. I'll send someone back with her and the necessary parts for repair of your wagon. This man needs to see a doctor."

"What's your name?" the glass man asked. "I mean besides the Alabaster Kid."

"Nothing impressive." I kept my back to him, but my senses were alert as I tied off Ferrell and loosed the horse. "It's not something you need to know."

"After all this, I think you at least owe me your name."

"All this?" I turned and tucked my hat down even more. "All this? What, did I disturb your quiet evening by saving your life? Did you know that this wanted fugitive was about to ambush you?"

"Well no, I..." He puffed his cheeks. "What I meant was..."

"Once his brothers find out he's missing, they will most likely come looking for him." I took a step towards the fire and lifted my head ever so much. "Why do you think he was out here tonight?"

He backed away and nearly tripped on a tuft of prairie grass. He caught himself with the butt of his rifle and stood back up.

"I imagine he was looking for folks like me who might be out late on the road," he said.

"More likely, he was looking for folks like me." I took a deep breath of the night air mixed with the warmed smoky waves from the campfire and the burnt beans on an open flame. "For folks exactly like me, really. His family came up from Appalachia during the war. They were the buzzards of the battlefield, thieving from the dead and dying, moving on every few years. I put away a couple of his cousins a few months ago, Zakk and Tommy Griller. The Ferrell boys broke Zakk out and ran off with him. Don't ask me why they didn't take Tommy. He was probably in no shape to travel. I got word that they were holed up near Veil. They had to know I'd come after him."

"Arthur Severin," the glass man said as he lowered his rifle to his side.

"How'd you hear of me, Arthur Severin?" I squatted near the flames and pretended to warm my hands. Truth was, I could barely feel the warmth I reached out for.

The glass man swallowed hard as he saw my long thin fingers and the blood-stained nails sharpened to a point, "Newspapers, telegraph… They say…"

"You shouldn't listen to the things *they* say." I stood back up. "People like to tell stories and when they don't have all the answers, they make some facts up to fit the stories they tell."

"I'm a writer," he said. "Well, I want to be."

"Then tell the truth, glass man." I walked back over to his horse. "What's her name?"

"The horse?" He walked towards me. "It's not mine. It belongs to the company."

"The glass company?" I ran my fingers across her brand. I had studied the annual brand books. "Is the federal government selling horses to glass companies now?"

"I don't..." He looked around. "How... Why do you think that?"

"Modified U.S. brand," I said. "So either the government owns this horse, or sold it, or it's stolen."

"I wouldn't know anything about it." He casually brought his rifle back up in front of his body but didn't point it. "I just..."

"You're just the glass man," I said. "You know the problem with glass, right?"

"Yeah," he said as if it was an afterthought. "It breaks."

"No," I said. "The problem with glass is that you can see right through it."

"Says the man who masks his face," he said back. "What are you hiding?"

"I hide in the night." I walked off. "You can't see through the night."

I led the horse into the darkness and met up with New Moon. About a mile out from the camp, Ferrell woke up and started screaming. I wondered if the glass man could hear him in the thin air. Hopefully, that would keep him on guard because if the glass man could hear the screams, then there was a good chance that other people could too.

CHAPTER FOUR

The rags began to itch, not because there was something inherently amiss with the new wrapping, but because of the anticipation. I could feel a tickle at the back of my neck, next to my knife. It was a heat from several sources, the heat of the oncoming day, the oncoming confrontation, the oncoming town.

Oleander told me about the Ferrell boys hiding out in Kansas and before he even said the name of the town, I knew it was Veil. Veil had sent a couple of killers at me a few months before the Grillers. It was like it had been calling to me, daring me to come, and now it was getting its wish. Oleander knew about this. Why else would he seek out the 'demon bounty hunter'? After hearing where they were, my curiosity was naturally piqued. I knew the Kansas terrain, and Oleander knew he would get his man... and his ten percent finder's fee.

I would have to find a place before daylight arrived, maybe a hotel. I've been known to bed down in ditches or mines. I wasn't sure exactly what I would find in Veil. The map I had was rough. Not a lot was known about this town, or advertised. Perhaps that is why it attracted the kind of men I was out to hunt down. There was certainly not much written even about its founding just after the war. There should be a book written about situations like this. Bounty men should not have to go in unprepared without proper study.

Books have always had high value in my life. They were my escape from reality and my salvation and my grounding in the same reality. They helped me better deal with the judgement of other people and understand the narrow minds that sometimes drive crowds into a fear-intoxicated frenzy. Books have seen me through bad days and empty nights. I can peer into the soul of a book and not worry about it looking back in expectation. Books accompanied me through the many destructive days I was forced to endure in dusty corners and dark ravines in order to escape being ravaged with burns. I learned long ago that it wasn't the heat that hurt me though. I could withstand the kind of temperatures that would immobilize a normal man. I could bathe in near boiling water. I could sleep in a blizzard. No, it wasn't the heat. It was the light. The purity of the light was like acid to me. It peeled away my mottled skin like the bark of a birch tree. It cracked and broke me. The life-giving light from Heaven was my Hell.

This is why I traveled at night. The near treeless prairie was as bad as a desert; it offered little protection. Its miles of flat grasses gave few places for shade. I hated hiding from the sun. My wraps helped keep me alive and mobile. The bill of my hat and my dark spectacles salvaged my white eyes. Still, even before it would rise, I could feel the light of the sky scratching to get at me, clawing at the gauze that was once my mother's petticoat, hoping to take advantage of a loose knot or a misplaced layer. The peculiar part is, I want so very much to let the light wash over me. I want to feel its acceptance. I crave its caress, yet I know I'm not worthy.

There is something unholy inside of me. It shows on my countenance. These rows of sharpened teeth clatter like the hanging knives in the butcher's shop in First Light. Mr. Crenshaw kept the knives in the shop as sharp as the ones he kept in a linen-lined drawer at the funeral parlor. My teeth always stayed sharp. My eyes cast an unearthly blue glow in the night, a reflection of the moon perhaps. They let me see like a wildcat in the near total darkness but caused me to turn away from the light and its purity. My ears are brought up to a point like the devils in the pictures in the Bible my original family left behind. I can hear the slightest rustle of leaves, the faintest footfall. Are these defects a clue as to my origin? Are they relics of a curse? I may never have the answers although I pray without ceasing as we are instructed to do.

There is plenty of time on most occasions to do that. I tend to travel by horse and avoid the congestion and questions on trains and coaches. Tonight I am pressed for time, racing the rising of the sun and the setting of a man's life. The few times Ferrell stirred, I tried to engage him. I was never much on conversation. There were not many who would seek to converse with me. It wasn't like in all the books. In my case, it often led to confrontation. Curiosity often breeds rudeness. The wrappings help. They are not nearly as obtrusive as what lies beneath, staring out an unforgiving mirror of accusation.

When I tell people that I was in a fire, that generally satisfies them, and it sounds better than admitting that I am a horribly disfigured demonic looking bounty hunter on a mission to capture or possibly kill a man. Plus, it's mostly true. I've been through the fire and flames, and it took much from me. I can explain myself much more clearly in writing. At times of convenience, I keep a journal. That is my conversation, my statement. It's not for any grander purpose of publication or pronouncement, but perhaps it will live on long after the bullet takes its pay. I just pray that my Savior sees enough light in me that I may enter His place with a new body.

My earliest journals were full of innocence at the remarkable world all around me and of the evocative imagery I found in the books from my trunk: Shakespeare, the Bible, Homer, and many more. I wrote in tiny script with a homemade pen on pieces of scrap paper that I bound in a booklet with rawhide. Although I wasn't allowed in town, Mr. Crenshaw let me come around at night and haul garbage that accumulated behind the butcher shop to the burn pile. As payment, I got to keep the torn or unused or discarded wrapping paper I found in the trash. I didn't realize until much later that he often added extra paper to the pile. The time I uncovered a nearly new roll of brown wrapping paper was like Christmas Day.

Those early years, even with the social fear and hatred by the townsfolk, were filled with the best times of my life on this earth. Instead of letting the dread and angst take over and consume me, my journal was filled with things like the shape and feel and sounds of a leopard frog in the creek in the back woods, or how I would spend hours at night practicing animal calls until I could match them perfectly. Each animal was a friend who never judged me, who feared only out of ignorance and never out of malice, because they were incapable of rational thought. I soon became a master mimic. At times it seemed like nature was actually answering me back.

All of those early crudely fashioned books were lost in the fire the night nature actually did answer back. It told me I was living in as much ignorance as my animal companions. There was no compassion to nature. She loved none of her subjects, least of all one so unnatural as myself. I was not her child, and she set out to prove it with an unholy vengeance.

The moans of Harris Ferrell took me from my reverie. These thoughts of the past always veered into territory untamed and dangerous. The now might seem more of a hazard, but I could lose myself in the past. The dark in those thoughts was way too black to see through.

It had been some time since Ferrell had made any substantial noise but the steady thrum of his breath and the obstinate beating of his heart along with the shish of the grass as we made our way through the stretch of prairie outside Veil had lulled me away into myself. No doubt I would be waking the sheriff just as the sun was awakening itself. I made my way through a well-kept field of corn. The greater portion had begun to be shocked by the intrepid farmer, like a hundred tiny

17

teepees. Soon it would be harvest, and it seemed like the season had been kind this year. It takes many backbreaking hours to work this land. Oftentimes the whole community banded together to help in times of harvest. It was amazing how an entire group of people could decide to do something as one.

A covey of quail jumped up from the grass and flew in front of me at the edge of a stand of trees. It was the time of the morning when the light could be seen in the distant sky, but it hadn't quite reached the ground yet. I stopped the horses. Why had the quail flown in front of me? It would have been more natural for them to fly away from me, leading me away from the nest. I listened. I scanned the tall grasses at the edge of the corn. I peered deeply into the recesses of the woods, deeper than most men could see. I saw nothing and I heard nothing unnatural, until I heard the cocking of a gun practically dead under my horse.

CHAPTER FIVE

I fell off my horse. I tumbled down behind New Moon, putting him between me and the Indian kneeling on the ground not twelve feet away from me, aiming his Remington at my head. Even as I fell, I pulled my left Colt out and fired between New Moon's front and back legs. He remained perfectly still. It was something we had practiced. The horse with Ferrell on it whinnied and skipped to the right a few paces. I hit my mark dead on with the shot. The problem was the mark was no longer on my mark. I deeply wounded a few corn stalks and a mound of dirt clods. New Moon flinched. I looked up to see the barrel of a gun pointed down on me. The Indian was standing balanced on New Moon's back, one foot on the saddle, the other foot on the base of the mane. I let out a high-toned whistle in two short bursts, and New Moon reared up on his back legs. The Indian leapt and rolled into the tall grass. I whistled another tone, and New Moon trotted off into the woods, huffing the whole way.

I could see the Indian's rifle tip in the grass, but something wasn't right. It seemed that both of us could easily hide from most men in the predawn light, but only I could actually see us. He may move silently, but I could tell there was no mass beside his gun. It was a decoy.

Holstering my pistols, I walked towards the trap. I saw him in the tree branches ready to pounce when I got closer. I pulled both of my guns and pointed them right at him. The peeking sun was at his back, and I was in the open so he could see what I was doing.

"You shouldn't leave your weapon lying out like this," I said. "It'll rust something fierce."

Not wasting a moment, he let out a scream like a jackrabbit in a rattlesnake's mouth.

"Eeee-YAHH!" He sprung at me and grabbed on to both of my wrists. He landed right on top of me, pinning me to the ground.

"You did not shoot when you had the chance," he spit. "Why?"

"My mistake," I said.

"You will find this true." He pushed down harder, trying to get me to drop my guns.

I began lifting my hands straight up against his full weight. His eyes widened, and he looked back and forth and tried even harder to throw his weight against me.

"You are strong for a wounded man," he huffed.

"And you are well spoken for an Indian." My guns were nearly pointed at him.

"HUHKK!" He bashed his head against mine with such force that I saw colors. Like a slingshot in recoil, he sprang back off of me.

"Holy God!" I jumped up, dizzy and startled. My vision was momentarily blurred.

I swung my fists out in front of me to block any oncoming attack. Nothing came. I holstered my guns and held my head. I couldn't tell if I was bleeding but I knew I would have a knot the size of a hen's egg at the top of my forehead.

A retaliatory strike never came. My senses cleared, and I could hear moaning. At first I thought it was perhaps Ferrell, but as I searched, I found the Indian on the ground, head bloodied, moaning and rocking. I was going to need a lot of bandages tonight.

CHAPTER SIX

"I don't want to leave you out here all alone, all tied up," I said.

"You can untie me then," the Indian answered back.

He peered up with only his eyes, leaving his head partly bowed, trying to see the bandage wrapped around his head. It made his hair stand out funny. He seemed to be an older man, probably in his mid-thirties. He was pretty spry for someone of that age. He was dressed in leathers with his arms bare, and he wore black denim pants. He had a leather necklace with a dark withered claw on the end. It was like a perverse mockery of the small golden cross under my own shirt. The cross had been my mother's, but I had been her real burden. It was almost all I had left of her. I wondered if this scrap of animal had any similar meaning to him or if it was just part of some pagan ceremony.

I had him sitting in the grass with his legs out in front of him, tied at the knees and ankles, and his hands tied behind his back using the same knot I used for my rags. I would have to stock up soon on new material. The ones on Ferrell were bloody, and there was no way I was getting into the special wraps in the bottom of my saddlebag. It had been thirty minutes, and I was running low on time. I had used the respite to secure him and to get myself something to sustain my energy and reinvigorate myself.

"However I have to get this man to a doctor and send help back for a man stranded on the trail."

"It is a road," he said.

"What difference…"

"It hasn't been a trail in years," he sneered, "not since the telegraph came through, not since the railroads and the fences carved everything up."

"I'm just here to take this criminal to the jailhouse." I scooped some beans out of a tin cup and into my mouth. "If I don't get there soon, he will die."

"He is a Ferrell," the Indian said. "I would have words with him before he is delivered either to the jailhouse or to Hell."

I squatted down and looked him in the eye. "You know this man?"

"I believe he has something to do with the abduction of my… friends," he said.

"Well, you won't be getting much out of him in this state." I stood and tossed the bean juice on the ground. "He's about out of blood and water and time. Anything I force down his throat comes back up."

"You did this to him?"

I turned to look at Ferrell, whose breathing had become more shallow.

"He tried to attack me," I said. "I tried to only wound him, but there was a fire in my eyes."

"Obviously," the Indian said. "Was he holding a weapon with his thigh?"

The sun had risen, and the long morning shadows were just beginning to recede. I tucked my tin back into my bag and reexamined the blood-soaked leg of my captive. The second shot had gone a little wild.

"I need to get him to a doctor," I said.

"Wake him." the Indian raised his head. "I have a camp near here. I have bitter herbs that would help his wounds and bring him to his senses, and then far beyond those senses where the pain will not follow."

22

"You're in luck." I pulled my hunting knife from my saddle flap. "I don't think he'll make it to town, and I want him alive as much as you." I cut his hands free. "But if you attack me, I'll take the shot next time."

With his freed hands, he got out of the other ties before I could even cut them.

"That will not be necessary." He jumped up. "We are not at cross purposes. The morning light has revealed much."

I tucked my knife into my belt and felt to see if my bandages were all in place. "Let's get on our way. The sun will be full shortly, and I promised a man I would send help for him."

"Allow me my medicines, and we can administer them as we progress." he wiped the dirt from his legs. "It is not ideal, but I will have my answers."

"Fine."

"My name is Golden Claw." He walked down the hedgerow.

"I'm called the Alabaster Kid." I took the reins of both horses and followed behind him.

"Yes, I know." He looked back over his shoulder as he walked away. "I have read about you."

Throughout the final miles to Veil, Golden Claw attempted, sometimes quite vigorously, to interrogate Ferrell. Some of his medicines were applied directly to the wounds. Others were forced into Ferrell's mouth. Once, Golden Claw chewed up some black stringy plants and spit them into Ferrell's mouth. It was all to little avail but not without some answers at least. Ferrell seemed to relay that he had seen Golden Claw's friends but denied abducting anybody. It was difficult to decipher some of his rantings, which were mostly about spiders but occasionally about the darkness and monsters and other things. Golden Eagle would fly into a rage in his own language, spewing what must have been cuss words. I could feel the coarseness of the language without needing to understand it.

"Indian trade!" Ferrell lolled his head, "Spider, spider, spider!"

It sounded as if his uncle, Zakk Griller, was with them, maybe in a shack north of town. Then he denied it all and started talking spiders again. By the time we reached the empty telegraph station just overlooking Veil, Ferrell was all spiders all the time.

"He is flying now," Golden Eagle said. "He will be this way for hours, and then the pain will return."

"If he lives that long," I said. "The pain might kill him when it comes back."

"I'm not entering the town." Golden Eagle stopped. "I will search to the north for these brothers and for Griller, and for my friends."

"If you let me know what you find before taking any action, I'll search you out and keep you abreast of anything I learn," I said.

"There is a reward for these men?" He checked Ferrell's rolled up eyes one more time.

"I thought your type didn't care about white man's money." I rearranged some of the bindings on the side of my face.

"You read too many dime novels." He smiled. "Sometimes the white man can only hear the red man through the gold man."

"No more than the fantasies you read about me." I looked up at the telegraph line, "Why didn't they take the line on into the town?"

"Perhaps there are things they do not wish to get out." Golden Eagle unlashed his rifle. He took a few steps then stopped and looked down. "I will not enter this town," he said, "unless I am deeply compelled, and then Veil will rue the compelling."

As he walked off, I looked over to where he had stopped. There was an old sign on the ground, nearly grown over and rotted.

VEIL, it read and below it, *Lamentations 3:65*.

I headed down towards the town. As I did, the scripture hung in my head. It was one of many I had memorized in my continual reading of the Word.

"Give them sorrow of heart, Your curse unto them."

As I reached the outskirts, there was a newer sign, a plain sign that simply read, *Veil*. There was no scripture written below, but I had a feeling that there was much more hidden underneath.

CHAPTER SEVEN

The mid morning sun was already high in the sky, and my headache was finally gone, literally and figuratively. I had dropped Ferrell off at the sheriff's office where it was confirmed, with much consternation, that the rest of the Ferrell clan had indeed chosen to set up camp somewhere outside of Veil. The sheriff was not a cooperative man. One would think that having your town plagued by outlaws would make one a little more receptive when one of those rogues was brought to the law. I did find out the connection between Griller and Ferrell. It was as I had heard. They were from a larger clan called Llatches. This familial band of rabble-rousers was known for its insurgence at least as far back as the War for Independence and definitely by the War of 1812. This family has been trouble in one way or another for quite some time. I guess the only thing they were better at than breaking the law was making babies.

I stepped out from between two buildings and wet a rag in a trough. For the first time, I noticed how rich this town appeared. The few people on the streets were dressed in fine clothes. The streets were swept cobblestone with built-in water runoffs along a finely decorated curb. The buildings were all fully painted, not just whitewashed, and many of them were brick. Each one had brightly colored trim and carved woodwork. A few of the two story buildings had gargoyles between their eaves. Even the bank had a decorated and probably fully functional parapet. Somewhere down the road, I could see construction and hear the hammers and saws already well under way. This town had a new look to it, but it wasn't new. This felt more like a facade, and I should know.

I backed back into the morning shadows that hadn't yet left the alleyways and leaned up against a damp brick wall. I peeled the wraps from my face and applied the cool wet rag to my forehead. I let out a sigh, and an irritating purr rose from the middle of my throat and up into my sinuses. I usually just shut down the unhuman noises my body occasionally tried to make, but I allowed myself a brief moment to feel the cool. I had to totally relax to feel it. I slid down the wall and sat on my haunches. The tension flowed from my shoulders. Cold never bothered me. In fact, heat never really bothered me, but to enjoy the embrace of either one, I had to completely surrender myself to the feeling. It was just that sometimes, when I did so, I was subject to the flames, the mocking, rising flames of so many years ago that still burned in my mind. There was no amount of wet rags that could smother those flames. Then I would shut them out and feel nothing again. The screams would cease, and my mother's voice would be quizzing me over my mathematics book, or telling me and my brothers to take the rough housing outside, or a thousand other mundane things, ending with the time she was doctoring my face after I had been in the sun too long. She held my blistered cheek in her cool hand, as cool as any compress, and she looked into my blank eyes and told me how much she cared for me and loved me. And I knew it was true. This memory was much happier than the last time I saw her face, though no less loving.

I heard the clopping of hooves on the cobblestone, and that's when I realized something. "Manure," I said out loud. The streets were too clean.

I took my fresh wrappings out of my bag and threw the old ones in. I took out my red sun cheaters and hung them on my belt. If I was going out into the sun, I would need them. I

27

made a mental note of a half-full barrel of rainwater that looked fresh. I could wash my old wrap here if necessary. Sometime I would have to replace what I lost the night before.

I looked out across the way to see the sheriff's boy, Jimmy Plummer, leading Severin's wagons into town. Their horses were the only ones in the street. There was no evidence of any other horses traveling anywhere else in town. That's why the streets were so clean. Then how did they get their goods and services around town?

A few people on the sidewalk balked at the sight. One man tapped his cane in disapproval. The woman he was with huffed and slammed the door to the bank as she went inside. The unwelcomed parade continued to the worksite at the end of the street. The glass man was delivering his goods.

I tied my wrap off and slipped my sun cheating specs over my eyes, tucking the temple ends between the wrap above my ears. This gave the town a reddish hue, but it protected my eyes from the sun.

I ducked around the back of the building and got at least one of my questions answered. There were several horses at different stations on a dirt road that encircled the city. I must have crossed it when I came into town earlier that morning, but I didn't pay it any special attention. Two men at the next building to my right were doing a familiar chore. One man was loading crates of salted meat onto a wagon, and the other was processing a hog for rendering. I spent many hours for many years up to my neck in entrails. One can learn a lot living with a butcher's family.

A woman stood with her hands on her hips. She was hovering over the man with the boxes. "How much longer are we going to have to do this black work?" She flung her arms around.

"I don't see you doing anything of the sort," the man grunted as he packed another crate onto the wagon.

"Shut your fool mouth, woman!" The rendering man looked up at me. "Mornin'… stranger."

I had been standing and staring like some sort of mute idiot.

"You, uh, hungry?" the man said. "Seeing all this pork can make a man crave his bacon."

"No, I…" I tipped my hat and walked past them. "My apologies. I used to, um…"

The woman girded herself and stepped back into the doorway as I continued down the row. Several buildings had horses tied out back. I had stabled New Moon inside earlier so he could get some food and rest. He hadn't been too happy about that. He preferred being outdoors at night. Even if the weather was inclement, we could always find some sort of shelter. Well, we could almost always find it anyway. Sometimes we were our own shelter and more than once, he kept me from frying in the light of the sun.

There was a man behind the blacksmith shop struggling to pull a mule in through the large wooden double doors. He was a small man on a futile task. He jerked and yanked on those reins with no progress at all. The mule obviously had no intention of complying.

"Do you need some help?" I approached the sweaty, tired little man.

"Only if you can convince a mule-headed mule to do somethin' it don't want to do!" He puffed his cheeks, dropped the reins, and jerked half-heartedly on a short rope around the animal's neck.

"Where's the blacksmith?" I looked in the doors.

"I own this shop!" he said with an indignant air.

"I never meant…" I had met a lot of blacksmiths, but never one with uncalloused hands.

I approached the mule with my hands up. The animal sniffed at me. Its cheeks quivered, and it looked away.

"I know," I said in a soft voice that I reserved for animals. "Ya-ya-yayaya…"

I touched her nose with one hand and the back of her neck with the other. I whispered softly into her twitchy ear.

"Ya-ya-ya… Come this way… It's okay… Yayayaya…"

After a minute of two, the animal looked into my eyes. I took off my spectacles and placed them on a loop at my belt. I pushed forward ever so slightly at the base of her neck. She took a step forward. For a moment, she hesitated as if she had startled herself.

"Come along, Jenny," I whispered.

I took the rope from the man's hands.

"She doesn't like the rope," I said.

"He wiped his hands on his shirt and then blew on them. "Sometimes the rope is necessary though."

"Not this time." I gently pushed the back of her neck and led her into the building.

There was quite a setup inside with evidence of more than just iron working tools. There were chains hanging from the rafters and a couple of open vents in the roof. Multiple hammers and different types of ovens lined the large space.

"You run this whole place yourself?"

The man was very happy to get his animal inside. "Oh, it's usually fine," he said. "We'll be up and running again once we…" he froze and stood erect, "get the help back," he finished quickly. "You need to get along now. I got a lot of work to do. Much obliged for the help."

He turned to his fire and stoked it with the same vigor he had used on the mule. I stood in the front doorway and looked at the construction across the road. A large church was in the process of being put up. I could see through the skeleton that there were several mill wagons delivering lumber in the back from the river east of town. The map Oleander provided was crude at best. The mill was at Bonnie Creek, it was believed.

30

Out in front of the construction was Arthur Severin and his wagons. He and others were unloading several large crates from the back. Six or eight men helped him with the task. I put on my sun cheaters and headed out into the daylight.

"The glass man cometh," I said in lieu of a greeting.

"Indeed!" he responded with a smile. "You looking for a job?"

"I'm on the job," I said and patted the head of the lead horse. "Good job, Missy. That was some load you had to carry for me."

"I assume you mean Harris Ferrell." Severin handed some two-by-two rough cuts to a man behind him. "Set these beside the pallet. We'll need to level that second stack."

"A much more onerous delivery, I assure you," I patted her mane, "than delivering colored glass to a church in the middle of a prairie."

"Just doing the Lord's work." Severin offered his hand. "Thanks for sending help back."

His friendly gesture wasn't something I was overly accustomed to. So for a moment, I just looked down at his hand. Just before he withdrew, I reciprocated.

"No! Yes, of course." I was a little too eager to reach out. My long wrinkled fingers engulfed his normal human hand. I had forgotten my gloves. I made it worse by reaching out my other hand and grabbing the back of his hand. I over shook. I could tell by the way his shoulder jerked and his eyebrow arched. "I mean… naturally."

I felt a tickle of embarrassment behind my ears as he looked down at my hands. When he turned away, I was able to regain my composure.

"I'm here to deliver stained glass for the new church." He did that thing I've seen nearly everyone do after they have touched me. He almost imperceptibly wiped his hands off as he turned away. I'm not even sure he knew he was doing it, but I always noticed it.

"Did Ferrell make it to the doctor?" He looked out over the work area.

"He made it to the jail, and the doctor showed up, but I don't know the specifics." I put my hands in my back pocket. "The sheriff and I didn't get on too well. I was asked to leave with an IOU and no information as to the whereabouts of his brothers or Griller."

"Yes, well good luck." Severin yawned. "After I get this unloaded, I'm going to shave and eat breakfast and catch a few hours sleep, maybe not even in that order. You leaving town?"

"Not without Griller."

"Where you staying?" Severin raised his hand to a worker and jumped over to the back of the wagon. "Whoa, WHOA! That's caught on the sheet! Pull that nail out first." He walked back over to me. "Can't be too careful with glass."

"They have a glass blower here in town." I pointed my thumb back over my shoulder. "Pretty good setup too. Why would they ship in glass?"

"They really did ship it in," he crossed his arms and smiled, "all the way from Paris, France. Heck, it was leaded in New York City."

"Then why do the crates say, Washington D.C.?"

"Heh... Well, that's where I'm from, where the company's from, Chiseled Glass, I mean." He rocked back and forth in his boots. "The sheriff's boy, Todd, I think, works for the Feds in D.C. He got us the job."

"That stringy little thing that came out to get you last night? I thought his name was Jimmy."

"No, his other son," Severin said. "Well, I really need to get back to..."

"You'll need to see him," I said, "the sheriff. You'll be going to see him."

"I don't think I'll…"

"I shot Ferrell." I took Severin's arm below the shoulder. My fingers wrapped all the way around his arm. "You need to let the sheriff know what happened."

"Fine, I'll… fine." He looked down at my hand, more alarmed at my grip this time. "Just let me shave and…"

"Look, I wasn't exactly asked to leave like I said." I pulled him a step closer. "I was more asked to stay, if you know what I mean."

"Did he arrest you?"

"Not exactly," I said, "but he wanted me to spend the night in another cell. He wanted me to answer a bunch of odd questions, and he wouldn't give me access to Ferrell after the doctor arrived. When I declined his invitation, things got a little heated. I left just before the inevitable threat came and even then, he followed after me. I had to slip away."

"Good Lord, have you slept?" Severin said. "I mean, that could all be normal procedure, but still…"

"I don't need a lot of sleep," I sighed, revealing yet another of my differences. "I just need some information. Wouldn't you like to get some information too, glass man? I bet there's a few things you would like to find out."

"What makes you think…" he paused and then pulled his arm back out of my grip and straightened his sleeve. "As a matter of fact, I'm due to have dinner with the mayor and other prominent citizens tonight to celebrate the delivery of the stained glass. I'll see what they've found out from Ferrell. How can I get ahold of you?"

"Not to worry," I said, "I'll be there."

"In disguise?" He covered his eyes with his open fingers, "It's not like you can blend in, and I highly doubt you have an invitation."

"I don't need an invitation."

"Yes, well, I'm staying at a farm house just north of town. It's where the dinner is." Severin pointed. "The road leads right to it. It's the old homestead of Orvinda Fellows. The townfolks call her Mother Fellows. She's a city leader. She and her granddaughter run the whole place."

"They run the whole farm?"

"That's where I'm staying, is all," Severin said. "Now let me get back to my panels before the locals shatter them all."

"Where's the hotel?" I looked down the street.

"There is none." Severin stopped and turned back around. "That's why I asked where you were staying. This town has no hotel."

"Veil has no hotel?" I looked again just to make sure. "Where do the travelers stay?"

"Have you seen any travelers?" Severin said in a quieter voice than he had been using. "Those that are invited to stay in Veil stay with Mother Fellows. Those that aren't invited to stay in Veil don't."

"And what about those that are me?" I asked.

"Those that are you sleep with your horse, I guess."

"I've had worse company."

"Yes," he said, "I'm sure you have."

CHAPTER EIGHT

I did get some sleep but by afternoon, I had grown restless. I awoke to three large young locals actively not watching the stall that New Moon and I were sharing. I decided to head out. The sun was high and uncomfortable, even in mid autumn. The sun was always on the hunt for its victims. It hated giving way to winter. It quite liked me, because its light could burn me even in the cold of January. I pulled my collar up and put on my gloves and specs, and headed out the back door with New Moon. After the party this evening, I would explore up north a bit, up past Mother Fellows' farm. Rogues like the Ferrells could take advantage of the cover and the cellar larder. They could raid the pantry and threaten an old lady and her granddaughter into silence. They wouldn't need to start a campfire that could give away their location.

There were some small caves out east by the river. I could check them out and see if there was anybody hiding in them, see if they were even habitable or if anybody had been using them. Depending on what I found out from Severin about Harris Ferrell, I might not even need to go back into town at all. The good Lord knows they didn't want me there. In that way, they were much like all other towns. With my speed and tracking skills, I could cover a lot of ground in the next few days. Four men, and with Griller probably still slowed down due to injuries, couldn't stay completely quiet, not from me. They were bound to be leaving footprints somewhere. It's too bad they suspected I was on their trail. Otherwise I could take them by surprise.

I headed back out west to the telegraph station first. I wanted to let Oleander know I'd caught one of the Ferrells. Maybe his office could pressure the sheriff to make good on his IOU. With the money this town had, shaking loose fifty dollars shouldn't be that difficult. Of course, given that Griller escaped before his court date, they may insist on waiting until Ferrell made it to trial first. And to think, I envy those poor men who have bank liens on a little house and farm and a few pitiful livestock. I hardly need the grief. If I don't get paid, it's only me and New Moon that suffer, and I can take care of both of us pretty well on a budget only big enough for the bullets to fill a hunting rifle.

The telegraph station was closed but not locked. I wonder why a rich town like Veil wouldn't have a railroad depot. The tracks don't even come this way. According to the map, the closest depot is over in Briar Town nearly seventeen miles away to the south, and then Chum over twenty miles down the river.

I looked around the small shack. Dust covered almost everything except the operator's chair and the machinery itself. Since I was out of the sun, I sat down inside and waited. I closed my sun-tired eyes and allowed myself a midday torpor of sorts. It cleared my head and helped mend my body. I could feel the blood pumping under my skin. I could feel myself melting into the shadows.

"Spiders," I said after a few minutes, not knowing why I said it.

I was brought to alertness by New Moon's whinny. Walking up the path with a black notebook in his hand was a little portly man in a brown suit and a derby hat. He smiled up at New Moon as he reached the building.

"Excuse me sir, I, OH!" He opened the door and jumped. When he got a good look at me, he closed the door and stepped back outside. He stood there breathing heavily with his hand on the knob. After three long breaths, he opened the door once again. "Good afternoon, sir." He refused to look up and marched directly around the desk to his chair. He dropped the notebook on the desk, stirring up a pile of dust, "Oh, my…"

"I'm…"

"You will forgive the state of the station." He spoke in a high-pitched tone with a bit of a German accent. He clipped the ends of his sentences. "I have been extra busy as of late."

"A lot of telegraph communications going out?" I brushed the dust off the arm of the bench.

"This is not my only job, Mister Alabaster Kid." He almost looked at me. "One moment, please."

He set a sign up on his desk from out of the top drawer. It was along triangular placard that read *One Moment Please*. He turned the sign in the little window that faced the front of the building to *OPEN*. Then he pulled out a difficult bottom drawer and placed the little black notebook inside. This was the only time he looked me straight in the eyes. I took off my red specs, and he immediately looked back down. He spent a moment dusting things with his handkerchief until neither of us could breathe. He opened the window, and I stood and opened the door. We both took a few seconds to continue breathing. He sneezed and wiped his nose with his dusty handkerchief, which made him sneeze even more.

"Forgive me." He placed his face out the window.

"God bless you," I said back.

He sat back down, nearly exhausted. He started to wipe his brow, but stopped as the handkerchief neared his face. He thought better of it and placed the dirty rag back in his pocket. I gave him the note with the message for Oleander.

"Beautiful penmanship," he said off hand. "Who wrote it?"

"I wrote it." My jaw clenched.

He looked down at the note and back up at me. "Payment up front," he said. "It's policy."

I leaned forward and down on the desk in front of him. "Just because I look this way…"

"Let me interrupt you there, sir." He turned to the machine with my note. "While I will admit that you initially caught me off guard, my perhaps curt manner has little to do with your appearance."

"I'm not an idiot," I said. "You don't think I know when I'm being treated poorly? I am well read. I'm well spoken. I've learned multiple trades. I am well experienced in being treated differently and with unqualified suspicion, so don't try to humor me with half truths born out of fear and misguided hatred."

He sat up straight and placed my note on his lap. His mouth pinched up and he looked straight ahead out the window.

"Three years ago, I accidentally…" He cleared his throat and continued to look away. "There was a fire in my home. All was lost. My wife was amidst the flames and perished. I lost two well-bred boxers, all of my belongings, my writings, a few… servants, but my daughters lived. Both of them lived."

"All I'm saying…"

"We struggled for months just to keep them alive," he continued. "The flames had devastated them. Beyond their appearance, they had been scalded to the core of their souls. Their minds and hearts were burnt and blackened. Many in the town who were once fine friends turned away in revulsion. My eldest had been giving eyes to the sheriff's oldest boy, Todd, but that was soon over. Those sweet little towheaded girls of ten and fourteen were shunned by the very neighbors and friends who had once claimed to adore them. I know the harsh reality of shallowness, Mister Alabaster Kid." He shoved my money back across the desk, leaving a trail in the dust. Tears filled his eyes. "It's the livelihood of yours that I was addressing harshly, sir. I have had poor dealings with bounty hunters in the past. They tend to make their own laws and intrude upon communities that have become perfectly adept at making their own way. Take your money. I have no desire to keep it in my box. I will send your message at my own expense."

I looked down at the change, and he pushed it even closer to me. I scooped it up and put it in my pocket. I wanted to say more, but words didn't come out. Should I apologize? No, he obviously mistreated me! I wanted to tell him my story, my fires, but the time didn't seem right. Besides, he had already turned back and started the message. I opened the door and started to leave.

"Eighteen months," he said, never looking up, the tears falling off his red round cheeks. "They lived for eighteen months. Eighteen torturous pain-filled months."

"I'm... sorry," I said over my shoulder. "Burns are some of the most..."

"It wasn't the fire, sir. It was a deeper injury, and..." he snipped. "It was... They died of arsenic poisoning."

"They killed themselves?"

"That is what the coroner said." He sniffed. "I maintain it was still the fire, although a different one, a slow burn that no salve could assuage. Your message has been sent."

I started again to speak but instead I pulled my hat down and walked out into the daylight.

CHAPTER NINE

Fortunately, it got dark quickly that time of year. I left New Moon in a small clearing north of town and made my way on foot towards the Fellows farm. As I do with the trails, I followed outside the road in the brush and scrub, which helped to hide my presence. This road had been well kept with large stones along the edges at regular intervals and fully grown oak trees just off of either side, interspersed with sprawling maples that reached out high over the road and shaded it. The leaves were in full color and had only just started to fall. The various hues blended in with the late day sky until one could scarcely tell where the foliage ended and the heaven began. My brothers used to ask me to describe the colors in the sky. Where they could see some blues and reds with different shades of gray, I could see a resplendent painting filled with subtle color changes so numerous that we had to make up names for them like cherry blossom and fire ant and west creek blue. I still think of those names when I see those colors. There were dozens of them.

Three horses were hitched outside the front porch of the large southern style mansion. The house and yard were in perfect condition. The whole estate seemed to be well taken care of. The visitors must have just arrived, but I hadn't seen them on the road. Why hadn't their horses been taken around?

My friend and teacher, Bill Crenshaw, used to tell me there were places where you should turn the horse for home. Always be ready to leave in a hurry if necessary. With luck, I wouldn't have to even go inside. I had the wind coming in my direction. That was good. That would let me hear a lot better. Unfortunately, there were a couple of men on either side of the front door, and they were holding rifles. That greatly limited how close I could get.

As I concentrated, I could block out some of the unwanted clutter of sound. I heard voices, muffled at first, inside the house. I couldn't yet understand the men. A woman said, "…to excuse my cooking. It has been a while."

I needed to get closer. The large trees in the yard afforded me opportunities to blend in with the shadows. As I got closer, I recognized one of the men at the door as the sheriff's son who had gone out to fetch Severin. He was holding both hands up to his mouth like he was eating corn on the cob. I didn't recognize the other man but he had a badge on, so I figured he must be the deputy.

I made my way closer, but Jimmy made it abundantly clear that he was not eating corn on the cob. He started in to playing the most God awful squawking on a tinny mouth harp. It completely obscured the conversations inside the house. What bits I could make out between his blows and sucks didn't make much sense.

"Sears and Roebuck." The boy smiled.

"Can you get your money back?" The deputy frowned.

I wished he would shut up with that racket.

"Shut up with that racket, boy!" The sheriff stuck his head out the door. "We're fixin' to play Mother Fellows' new Victrola recording."

The music began indoors. The sheriff's son put his harmonica in his vest pocket and pouted. The music was a fast paced piano tune like the ones I had heard in the saloons and the doorways of large department stores in Kansas City. The deputy tapped his feet and smiled. Jimmy was a little more animated, stomping and clapping and whistling off key. I could hear nothing from inside aside from the music and the occasional clink of glassware.

As the boy, who was probably around my age, danced around in his chair, something around his neck jumped up and down and side to side. It was hard to see what it was because it was black and so was the kid's vest. The more I looked, though, the more sure I was that it was a bird's claw on a leather loop. By the time I was positive, I was already at the foot of the porch steps with my guns raised, not yet realizing what a stupid thing I was doing.

"Where did you get that claw?" I demanded.

"What the heck are you?" The boy fell over out of his chair.

The deputy stood and went for his gun. He had a rifle and a pistol.

"Don't!" I demanded and pointed my right Colt in his direction.

He froze.

"Give me that necklace." I looked at the boy.

He held the claw in his hand. He squinted and cocked his head.

"I just found it, is all," he said, "down near the Spider Caves. I didn't steal nothin'!"

I holstered my left gun and held out my hand, "Give it to me!"

I felt something slap around me like a limb from a tree as a large lasso wrapped around my chest from behind. I was so caught up in the moment, that I didn't hear someone coming up behind me.

"Got him!" a voice yelled.

The music stopped. The deputy lunged at me, and we both flew off the porch. I landed on my back with him on top of me. My arms were pinned to my side, and he managed to wrest my weapon from my hand.

"Go!" someone yelled as Jimmy tried to kick me in the ribs.

The night flew and tumbled all around me as the horse on the other end of the rope dutifully took off at full gallop.

"This must be the Ferrell brothers," I thought in between bumps.

Were they somehow working with the town? I tried to turn, but the ground and the large rocks battered me pretty badly. The rope only grew tighter as I struggled. There was a short pause as the horse changed direction. I felt the knot slip ever so slightly. I was swinging towards the base of a large oak tree. I needed to free myself now, or I might not get another chance. He took off with renewed spirit.

"Spider Caves," I thought as the tree smashed into my face.

CHAPTER TEN

People claim their blood tastes like iron. I never got that from mine. Mine always reminded me of persimmons, you know, slightly sweet, but with the type of sour that made you want to pucker until your cheeks ached. I don't know how long I had been puckering, but my cheeks ached most foul. There was a darkness I could not see through. I blinked several times, but was still blind. My arms were tied behind me, and I was seated in a wooden framed chair with no armrests. My feet were tied at my ankles. Everything ached but not as much as my head. The tree had been most unforgiving. My teeth all seemed to be in place but like I said, there was that distinct taste of persimmons. I could smell… fried chicken, I believe, and an array of side dishes. A little girl whimpered. There was the strangest click in my eyes that I had never felt before and a feeling as if mud had been dug from the sockets all at once. I can't describe the next sensation any other way, but it was like I opened my eyes twice without closing them in-between. Voices mumbled, but I could barely make sense of my own thoughts, let alone dialogue from across a room. A brown haze of light became visible. Someone had placed a burlap bag over my head. No wonder it was so difficult to breathe.

"He's movin', Pa," the sheriff's boy said.

"Get 'im up." The sheriff's voice sounded like the rocks I had been drug through. "I need to have words with this sidewinder."

I had never been called a sidewinder before—a rattlesnake many times, a bat occasionally, but never a sidewinder. That had implications beyond my physical appearance. I was lifted to my feet by two men, one on either side. The chair was kicked away behind me. The men grabbed my arms above my elbows and jerked. Then they dragged me across the room. One sleeve, my right, was torn and probably bloody from the feel of it.

"God, what's wrong with his arm? He got some kinda' disease?" the man on my right said. "I gotta go wash my hands."

"Stay put!" the sheriff ordered from in front of me.

I was starting to take account of my surroundings with the aid of my other senses. The sounds of plates in front of me, the smell of food, told me I was probably in the dining room. I could hear the girl, probably the granddaughter of Mother Fellows.

"What are you going to do with him?" the voice of Arthur Severin spoke next to the sheriff. I think they were across from me at the dining table.

"You stay put!" the sheriff said to the man on my right.

"Sheriff!" the man whined.

There was no fire in the room, so they must not have lit the fireplace yet. It couldn't be much later than when I went under. I could smell and hear the gas chandelier above me. This must be a grand room. The man on my left pulled the bag off my head, and the world went white. In less than the tick of a clock, it seemed like someone placed smoke colored shades over my eyes. I was able to see through a haze. Everyone pulled back and gasped. The little girl screamed and hid behind her grandmother. They were standing across a large dining table still filled with food. My guns were also on the table, right in front of the sheriff. The people all stared at my face as the gray shades slowly pulled back like blinders on a horse.

"What… what manner of beast are you, boy?" The sheriff seemed genuinely perplexed, not like he was just throwing out some insult.

The men at my sides looked nearly identical in all brown baggy shirt and pants and farmer hat. Even though they were armed with shotguns, they pulled back in fear. I wasn't sure what was happening. No one was holding gray colored shades. The men raised their shotguns. My wraps were still in order, although bloodied, I'm sure.

"Pull those rags off." The sheriff pointed at me. "I wanna know what we're dealin' with here. Just what in tarnation has the government been up to now? They sending us demonic agents?"

"I ain't touching him." The man on my right sighted me through his gun and stepped back one step.

The sheriff looked to the man on my left, "Glenn?"

"Not on your life." Glenn raised his hands and shook his head. "Yer honor?" Glenn looked at the man at the far left end of the table. It was the man from the telegraph station.

"Well, I… I, I…" he stuttered and looked down at the table.

"Hold yer pie, Ned." The sheriff raised his hand. "I…"

"I'll do it!" The sheriff's son Jimmy was waving his hand over by the side exit. He twiddled with the claw in his other hand.

"You settle down too, Jimmy." The sheriff put his arm on an old lady to his left. "We got women folk here. You might wanna take Cherish in the other room, Mother."

"Not in my house, I won't," the old lady said. "Sides, I'm just as curious as you-all are."

"Let me do it, Sheriff Plummer." Severin, who was just to the right of the sheriff, spoke up, "And you might be right about getting the women out of here. I've heard stories about the Alabaster Kid."

"I thought he was a bounty hunter, not a federal lawman," Sheriff Plummer said. "Either way it was him what trespassed on private property and drew a pistol on a deputy sheriff."

That was the one unaccounted for, the deputy.

"You men need to stand back." Severin came around the end of the table. "He's dangerous when he's caged."

The two men moved back as Severin walked up in front of me. He turned around and pushed my guns back on the table towards the sheriff.

"It's like you got two eyelids," Severin got in my face and examined my eyes, "like some kind of lizard."

Oh, I had gotten "snake eyes" and "goat eyes" and "demon eyes" all my life because of the unique shape of my pupils. I often wondered how any of them knew what a demon looked like. Most of them had never even seen the renaissance masterpieces that I had read about in my treasure chest of books. The two eyelid thing was new and different though. That oak tree must have knocked something loose.

"Now, why would Washington send out a federal agent to this sleepy little town in Kansas?" Severin walked to my side and kept looking at me.

"We ain't done nothin' wrong!" Jimmy Plummer pointed at me.

"Hesh up!" the sheriff said. "Let's see it, Severin."

Severin reached over to the table and picked up a sharp steak knife. He wiped it on his sleeve.

"Hey, glass man," I said. "Told you I didn't need an invitation."

"That you did." He placed the flat of the knife against my cheek. "That you did."

He pulled something out of a hole in the bottom of my vest pocket. It was my red specs. One of the lenses came off in his hand. He placed the lens and the frames in his side pocket.

"Not sure you'll be needing these again."

He walked around behind me. The coterie on the other side of the table stared on. Mayor Telegraph Man pulled at his collar and wiped his brow with a clean red handkerchief.

"There is a braid in the back." Severin pushed my hat forward, almost covering my eyes.

I felt his knife at the base of my neck. He cut through one wrap and tossed each end over my shoulders. He stopped short when he got to my hidden knife.

"Is the skin on his neck like his arm?" the man in brown that had been on my right said.

"He's pretty beat up, Mother Fellows," Severin said. "Are you sure you don't want to fetch some water?"

"Soon enough," she said.

As he spoke, he slid the thin blade of mine down the outside of my duster between my shoulder blades. With his knife, he popped another wrap loose, revealing my lower jaw and sharp teeth. I hissed, and the little girl screamed and fainted into her grandmother's arms.

"Get her out of here!" the sheriff ordered.

As she fainted, Severin slipped the blade into my hands. My long fingers were able to manipulate it in a way most men could not. He pulled at the ropes.

"Are these tight?" He looked over to Jimmy who was creeping forward. "Stay back! I've seen him pick up a man one handed and throw him up on a horse. What have we here?"

He knelt down to the ropes tied tightly at my ankles. His knife started cutting through the knot as he pretended to retie it.

"Nice try, demon spawn!" He loosened the ropes, but held the ends together. "You just about freed yourself. We need one of you over here right now. Glenn?" He let go of the ropes around my ankles, "I said NOW!"

I spun around and flung my hands free. I grabbed Severin by the shirt and threw him across the table at the sheriff. I pushed Jimmy out of my way as I headed for the doorway. The men in brown raised their shotguns to fire. Mother Fellows clutched at her granddaughter. The mayor ducked down below the table.

"Don't shoot!" Severin cried out as he blocked the sheriff and gave the men a moment's pause. "There are innocent people in here!"

I fled through the door into an entrance hall. The stairs and a hallway were to my left. Another room was in front of me, but the open front door to the cool night air was to my right. As I approached the door in a sprint, the deputy turned into the doorway from the porch. His gun was raised. I jumped as soon as I saw him. I crashed right through the large window beside the door. He turned and shot at me and grazed my back at my shoulders. Searing pain like the sun on a summer's day sliced through me. I had no idea how deep the shot was. My muscles tensed and allowed me to nearly fly off the porch into the darkness with mighty leaps that no man nor beast could follow. Once the shadows had me, I was gone. That may have been so, but it sure wasn't going to stop them from trying their best to catch me.

CHAPTER ELEVEN

My brothers both owned beaver coats. They trapped the beavers themselves. Sammy was an exceptional trapper, and Benny could skin a cat faster than you would believe. I learned a lot from them, but I never owned a beaver coat. It wasn't just because beavers were scarce, it was more because I just didn't need one. On cold, cloudy, snowy days, I would trudge through the snow with my brothers, gathering wood or hunting small game. They were tucked and rolled in furs and rags to protect them from the cold. I would be barefooted and not even wearing a shirt. Back then I was invincible, or at least I pretended to be. I was chilly, especially during those below zero days when the snow was as dry as powder and wouldn't pack. I just liked showing off.

"Why don't you breathe some fire and warm this place up?" Benny laughed.

"How about I just burn you up?" I breathed out my steamy breath at him.

"No, I will!" Sammy breathed at him too.

Soon we were all standing around blowing 'smoke' at each other in the frigid January air until Father walked past us with a load of firewood in his arms.

"Save some of that energy for carrying wood," he said and trudged off towards the house, puffing his own clouds of breath.

It was a miracle of days when I was surrounded by a normal human family that treated me just like one of them.

"Come on!" Benny said. "There's a dead pine down at the creek. We can bust off some branches."

Well, you give three boys long sticks to play with and the whole world becomes a sword fight. Up and down the steep banks, we swatted and smacked each other.

"Hah!" Sammy swung around a snow-covered mound of dead prairie grass.

I was completely ready for him. I blocked his swing with my arm and poked him in the chest with my stick.

"Hah!" I shouted back.

"Whoa!" He swung his arms around in circles and dropped his stick.

He was slipping in his beaver skin boots and was losing his balance on the top edge of a limestone cliff. Below him, about twelve feet down, was solid ice punctuated by shards of pointed rocks. I threw my stick away and leapt in his direction. I don't know how I found purchase, but I grabbed him by his coat and flung him up the cliff into the grassy snow. However, I then had naught but air to cling to. Flapping like Sammy had just been, I seemed to take flight. The sky was a dull gray as I fell down, face up. White and then black accompanied a sharp crack between my shoulders as I landed on sharp rocks and hard ice. It seemed the ice had pierced my soul. Instead, the rocks had cracked at least one rib.

For two days, my mother plied me with melted snow water and chicken broth. On the third day, I was famished. I ate everything she brought me. Whole jars of canned vegetables vanished down my gullet. I could and would have eaten the bark off a tree if I had been given the chance. I scoured through the woodpile for insects to gobble up. Father complained that we would be eating the horse before spring if I didn't slow down. When Sammy brought in a possum he killed, I could scarcely wait for it to be cooked. They let me eat the whole greasy thing myself. We usually only ate possum in times of need, and Father agreed that this qualified. By the fourth and fifth days, I was up and as strong as ever. Mother thanked the Lord, and Father espoused the power of prayer. Sammy claimed his possum was lucky. I remember them all huddling around me in a big family hug. Then Father told me if I was feeling so mighty, I should go split some wood, and that's exactly what I did.

As I opened my eyes to the now, the world made little sense to me. I could still feel their arms around me as I realized they were my own arms. The shapes in the night were all wrong, but I was hanging upside down like a bat from the branches of a large tree. My hat was below me on the leafy ground. Drops of blood dripped from the top of my head. I held the bent barrel of a shotgun in my hand. Great Father in Heaven, what had I done?

A light through the trees about thirty feet away told me that someone not too smart was meandering this way. There was a cold painful line across my back and shoulders. I rolled my shoulders, but the line remained, and the pain increased. Directly across from my tree was a large dead pine tree. Branches had been broken off from the ground to about eight feet up. From the smell of the pine tar on my hands, it was obvious that I had done it. The man with the light made his way unerringly between the two trees. He stopped and looked down at my hat. A drop of my blood hit the top of his lantern and sizzled. He looked up as I fell down upon him.

I knew now. I knew how to twist in the fall and land on my feet. I practiced it often after the accident in the snow. By the time spring arrived, I was showing off my new skill, leaping backwards off of Peter's Cliff and landing on my feet between the rocks, safely sinking to my ankles in the pebbles, sand, and silt. Sammy said we could make a fortune in New York City. Benny made me do it over and over until I was exhausted.

I landed solidly behind the man with the lantern and the shotgun. I figured he or his identical brother must have been the ones who lassoed me.

"Hah!" I clipped him in the jaw with the bent shotgun barrel I carried.

He and his shotgun and his lantern fell into the leaves and the broken branches next to my hat. The lantern went out. I put my hat on the blood soaked rags wrapping my head. I pulled them off and threw them on the ground. I put my hat back on and tightened the drawstring below my chin. I carried the man to the dead pine, lifted him up off the ground by his shirt and hung him high on a broken branch by his jacket. One of his teeth fell out of his mouth.

"I am sorry," I said to the unconscious man, but I wasn't sure I really was.

Only the night breeze answered back, but in the distance, I could hear what I believed to be footfalls. I was still disoriented. I wasn't sure which way New Moon was. I took a gamble and ran off away from the footsteps. I soon found myself at the edge of the woods, back at Mother Fellows' mansion. At least this let me reset my compass. I now knew where I was. I turned to the road and saw Mother Fellows standing there looking at me and my unwrapped face.

"You gonna kill an old lady?" She was holding one of my Colts to her side.

I froze for a moment. She looked over to her porch.

"Come on inside," she said. "I'll get you a drink."

I raised the shotgun at her. She closed her eyes and dropped the Colt.

"Ya' cain't fight the U.S. government," she said. "I learnt that years ago. It'll just take everthing ya' got and grind it inta' mush."

"I just want to go." I walked up and took my gun off the ground. It felt like my shoulder was tearing away from my body.

"You go now, you'll be shot 'for dawn." She opened her eyes. "Then we'll be havin' a hunnerd federal monsters down on us."

"I'm not…" I wondered if Oleander had set me up for this.

"If'n I help you out, maybe you won't lock me up and take my home… again."

I looked into the woods. They seemed darker than usual against the lights hanging on the porch.

"How can I trust you?" I said.

"If the war taught me anything, it's that you cain't trust nobody. You just gotta take a chance sometimes, is all. 'Sides, you don't think you can stop an old lady?"

"It doesn't matter who pulls the trigger," I said. "A bullet doesn't care who shoots it."

"True enough." She started towards the house. "You can stay out here if'n you want, but I cain't help but noticed you followed me up on the porch here."

"Let's get out of the light," I said.

As we walked past the broken window and then the stairs to the back of the house, Mother Fellows whispered a short prayer under her breath.

"Lord, have mercy," she repeated over and over again.

I stopped in front of a wall-mounted mirror to survey the damage. There were multiple cuts through my torn shirt, my arms, chest, and face, and there were a few swollen places that hadn't been swollen before, and I was relatively sure should not ever be swollen. I couldn't see the deep gash under my torn and bloodied duster jacket across my shoulders, but I could feel it calling.

"Was this the devil or the state what done this to you?" Mother Fellows looked at me looking at me in the mirror. "Come on now."

She opened the cellar door that was built into the north wall of the house. The dank dirt smell wafted out into the room. I could see the flicker of a small candle somewhere below.

"Mind the jars along the steps," she said. "Those things ain't cheap, and I got more punkin and squash ta' can. There's an old army cot down there. I'll bring ya' a wash bowl down in a bit."

I looked off to the line of rooms down the hall to my left.

"Them's the bedrooms," she said. "This here's for you."

There was no lock on the door, and she wouldn't be able to move anything in front of it to block it that I couldn't move. I stepped down the stone steps until I was completely underground. All around me, flickering in the glow, were colored jars filled with a garden's bounty. How could one old lady put up so many goods and how would she eat them all in one winter? Sitting on the cot was a well-dressed man. He was holding my other Colt.

"Don't you just love the way the lights dance in the glass jars?" He looked at me.

"Glass man," I said.

"Want this?" He threw me my gun. "I think I have something else you might want."

I caught my piece and placed it in my holster. "What are you doing here?" I asked.

He held up Golden Eagle's claw necklace. "Little Jimmy Plummer has a big mouth. He said you tried to take this from him. I don't remember seeing this when we first met. Is this something you want?"

"I'll tell you what I want." I reached over him and grabbed a jar of pickled beets. "You think Mother Fellows knows how to cook possum?"

CHAPTER TWELVE

"You're back to the waking world." Severin tossed my duster on the broken dining room chair that had been brought down to the cellar.

I was seated on a now empty shelf carved out of the limestone shale, formerly used to store jars of vegetables. I sat legs crossed, wearing only a wrap to gird myself and my mother's golden cross around my neck. A new candle had just been lit, by the smell of it.

"I'm back?" I opened my eyes. "Where have I been all this time?"

"I may, in reality, be the real federal agent around here," he sat in another broken chair, "but I still have to oversee my stained glass church cover. You're in luck."

"How so?"

"Plummer won't send for official help." Severin turned an empty jar over in his hands and looked inside. "There are no more than a half dozen men out looking for you right now, although there may be several others coming in from neighboring farms and even other localities."

"Why do you suppose that is?"

"I'm still an outsider," he said, "but I'm asking around. I haven't heard a single thing about the Ferrells or Griller. I can't get access to the jailhouse either, not that it matters. My biggest worry is still finding concrete evidence of the slave ring we were tipped off about."

"How long have I been down here?" I rubbed my eyes.

"Just a few days," Severin said.

"Mother Fellows has sewn my clothes." I held up my shirt. "I am a patchwork man."

"She did a fine job on the duster." Severin nodded his head towards it. "That'll cover a multitude of lesser sins."

"All sins are equal in God's eyes," I said.

"The old lady seems to be keeping quiet." Severin pulled a pickle from an open jar. "Cherish too."

"The girl knows I'm here?"

"I heard she's been bringing down food." he smiled. "You can't tell the difference between an old lady and a girl?"

"I have been deep in prayer."

"We call that sleeping it off, where I come from." he took a bite of pickle. "Hmm. Slave labor can produce some mighty fine cucumbers."

"I have been in communion, then," I uncrossed my legs, "with the Holy Spirit. It has been healing me."

"From the looks of these bones down here, Mother Fellows has been feeding you AND the whole Holy Trinity, Mother Mary, and all the saints." Severin kicked some turkey bones away from his chair. "I've got something else for you."

He pulled a thin narrow wooden box from his vest pocket and set it beside me. I picked it up and turned it over in my hands.

"Open it up," he said.

"I fully intended to." I looked at him over the box.

"It's your glasses," he said before I even got the box fully open. "I fixed them."

"I see," I said. "Thank you."

"Those original lenses aren't glass," he pointed. "They're a cut stone. I'm not sure what kind. My skill is only in glasswork."

"And in framework too," I said as I tried them on. "They fit perfectly."

"Look," he said, "down underneath in the cloth are some other lenses. I made green and blue, another red and a kind of yellowish."

"Very nice," I said. "I appreciate it."

"Harris Ferrell is gone," Severin said and looked at the floor.

"What?" I jerked up and hit my head on the stone wall, nearly dropping my new specs. "Dead?"

"I don't think so. I can't get in to see." Severin slapped his thighs and sighed. "I've just been told he's gone and I don't need to worry myself about it. Plummer won't say any more about it. He just says he's been sent away and to mind my own business."

I stood up in the cramped space, but I had to stay bent to avoid hitting my head on the ceiling. I turned to pick up my shirt. Severin picked up the candle and brought it closer.

"Good Lord," he said. "I saw that wound when Mother Fellows was cleaning it. Now it's completely scarred over, and over here it looks like even the scar is going away!"

"Blessings and curses," I said. "I am ample with both. My cup runneth over."

As I turned back around into the light, Severin backed up a step.

"God," he said. "You are one scary hombre, all concerned. No offense."

I smiled. "No offense? That's good to know."

"I've not heard anything from this Golden Eagle Indian you talked about either." He sat back down. "You suppose they caught him?"

"It's unlikely they caught him unawares." I put the claw necklace over my head. "I think our answers lie in the Spider Caves."

"Yes, I've been trying to get over there, but they keep a close eye on me," he said. "I think I've wrangled a way to get up there this evening. A few of the men who are looking for you have spent a lot of time out there. As an outsider, I still can't get much out of them."

"That should tell you something." I buttoned my clothes.

"Oh, it does." Severin reached into a bag he had hanging on the back of his chair. "I was hoping you might want to come too? We've taken good care of your horse while you've been down here."

Severin pulled out a large spool and tossed it to me. It was wound with fresh clean linen that had been torn into a long strip of cloth. "Turns out, it's harder to hide a horse than a human."

I looked down at the spool. The whisper of a smile crossed my lips. "Just let me finish getting dressed," I said.

CHAPTER THIRTEEN

"What a fool thing to do," I said to the empty cellar. "Plummer sends Ferrell away, his brothers are bound to leave too. That does me no good at all."

Severin had left some time before. He was supposed to be back at sundown so we could check out the goings on at Spider Cave. If our assumptions were correct, Veil, Kansas was about to be in very big trouble. My main concern, though, was that the law and the Ferrells seemed to be working in concert. I first thought that the brothers and Griller were just hiding out in the outskirts of the town, living off the leavings. Then it came to me that perhaps they were holding a hostage, or somehow threatening the town. That would explain some of the odd standoffish behavior and the appearance of disinterest in their capture. Now I wondered if the sheriff might be in cahoots with the outlaws. The tendrils of the Llatches clan stretched deep into some of these middle American towns. It was how Griller escaped. He was kin to a guard at the jailhouse.

I went up to make some sort of payment to Mother Fellows. I didn't have a lot of money, but I had my IOU for bringing in Harris Ferrell. I owed her a great deal, even though she said she had only helped me because she thought I was a government agent, an idea that Severin apparently did not dispel.

I stepped out into the hall and closed the door behind me. There, at the other end of the hall, holding a doorknob to another room and wearing only a towel, was Zakk Griller. We stood there looking at each other in shock, both of us with our hand on our doorknob. He turned his hand and pushed. The door squeaked open to his room. Neither of us said a word. It was like we were watching a coiled rattlesnake at our feet. I turned my hand and pushed. My door squeaked open to the cellar. I kept my eyes on his eyes. We both took a large slow step in through our respective doorways and gently latched the doors behind us.

Run or fight, which would he choose? I could catch him right now if he was alone, but I didn't know who or what awaited me when I opened the door back up. The Ferrell brothers could be there, guns drawn, waiting to mow me down. I gathered my things in haste and put my hand back on the doorknob. What if they were now waiting outside this door? How many shots could I sustain before I either died or took them down with me? Was it even worth it?

"To rid the earth of even one more member of that evil family would be worth my own life," I said to the door.

With my guns in my hands, I swung the door open. No one was there. I stepped out. Every sense was on high alert, even senses I didn't know I had at the time. I crept down the hallway, glancing up and behind with every step. When I reached his door, I looked down at the glass doorknob. It was still. I saw no shadows on the floor through the crack at the bottom of the door. There was a trail of water leading to the room. There must be a washtub down the hall. I stood to the side of the doorway, somewhat protected by the jamb. I turned the knob and swallowed hard.

Nothing.

I flung the door open, expecting a hail of bullets. It slammed against the wall and cracked the plaster.

Nothing.

I heard no movement, but felt a breeze. He and/or they had escaped through the window into the blinding sun.

"Mother Fellows," I whispered.

"Mother Fellows!" I called as I ran to the other room, "Mother Fellows!"

I found her and Cherish in the sitting room, sitting. Cherish held a roll of yarn on her hands, and Mother Fellows calmly rolled a ball from it.

"Mother Fellows," I said, nearly out of breath, "Zakk Griller. He was here in your house... in a towel."

"Of course," she said. "If'n there's one thing you should have learned from me during yore stay, it's that I know how to treat family."

CHAPTER FOURTEEN

"I just left her there." I bent down in the undergrowth next to Severin. "What else could I do?"

"One crisis at a time, I suppose." Severin rubbed his chin and looked out at the overgrown caves in front of us. "This isn't right."

"From the looks of them, I'd say the Spider Caves are aptly named," I said. "I don't imagine many insects get past those openings."

"They're too shallow." He brought a brown folded piece of paper up out of his shirt pocket. "Overgrown like that, I doubt there are even bats inside. Here."

He handed me a crudely drawn map of the caves.

"Known officially as Bonnie Caves, they got their local name because of the shape." He continued to peer through the early evening darkness. "It won't be long before we won't be able to see anything."

The meandering system did bear a similarity to a large spider, albeit one with several broken legs.

"The dogs will find us before then." I handed him his map back.

"Those dogs are way off." He tucked the paper away. "Besides, what scent of yours do they have to follow?"

I ran my fingers over the claw around my neck. "How eager was the Plummer boy to hand this over to you?" I took the necklace off. "And those dogs are a lot closer than you think. They're a beagle mix mainly used to hunt coon. They won't attack us, but they already have a scent."

"How do you know?"

"I can tell," I said.

"I see you got my message," a voice behind us said.

Severin went for his gun. I already had mine drawn as we swung around.

"All right, mister…" Severin said.

"Hold on." I lowered my Colt and placed my other hand on top of his gun. "He's with us."

"You are in the wrong place," Golden Eagle spoke calmly. "It is one of the reasons the dogs haven't found you yet."

"This your Indian friend?" Severin looked at me and holstered his gun.

""The Ferrell brothers took some of his friends," I said. "He's been out here scouting for them."

"And I found them," Golden Eagle pointed to his right, "but this operation is much bigger than I expected. I've been gaining information for the last couple of days. It has been all I could do not to raid the compound, but I needed more information first and hopefully more allies."

"Tell us what you know." Severin placed his hands on his hips.

"Who is this white man?" Golden Eagle looked at me.

"He *is* an ally, but telling you who he is won't make you trust him any more," I said.

"I'm Arthur Severin with the United States Secret Service," Severin said. "We started out investigating a counterfeiting setup, but it turned into a possible illegal slave trade organization."

"Not just possible but true." Golden Eagle reached out and took the claw from my hand. "And yes, knowing who you are only makes me more wary of you."

"I think they have the claw's scent," I said.

"Head towards the dogs." Golden Eagle put the claw around his neck. "I will lead them away."

"What did you find out?" I looked down the direction he pointed. There were several hills that must have held the Spider Caves.

"We can trust this man?" Golden Eagle tightened his lip and looked at Severin.

"I don't see another choice," I said.

"Thanks," Severin said.

"I have other choices," Golden Eagle said.

"Trust him," I said. "I can see through him."

Golden Eagle sighed. "There are dozens of black men, women, and children in the main chamber," he said. "It is only lightly guarded, but the men are shackled to the wall."

"Good Lord," Severin shook his head.

"My... friends are in this chamber as well." Golden Eagle's eyes grew dark. "To the right of the entrance is a large tunnel that leads to two more holding areas. They have been turned into cells. One cell holds three black men. The other holds two white men. I have not spoken to the white men, but the black men were placed there after severe beatings. They attempted to escape recently when all the town's slaves were brought in."

"Wait," I said, "you were inside?"

"Why were the slaves brought here?" Severin reached out his hand. "What's changed recently?"

"They knew you were coming." Golden Eagle frowned at Severin. "That's probably why my people were taken, to keep anyone from talking to you. If only I hadn't been out hunting..."

"They didn't know I was coming," I said, "and they think I'm the agent."

"They knew I was coming..." Severin looked off in thought. "They set it all up through Todd Plummer, the sheriff's oldest boy. He works for the agency and came to us to report this whole thing to begin with."

"Some sort of reverse agent?" I said.

"But why?"

"Who knows." I looked at them both. "When men leave home, they often try to rid themselves of the wrongs inherited by their fathers, but oftentimes their fathers can have a deep hold on them, even halfway across the country."

"No, I mean, why don't they know I'm the agent?"

"Oh."

"If Todd wired his father that I was coming, why didn't he say who I was?"

"Maybe he *does* know." Golden Eagle stood up from the brush and checked his pack. "Perhaps he is duplicitous."

"Someone is," I said.

"The three black men are very brave." Golden Eagle produced a rough looking key from his bag. "Jed, Lincoln, and Everett. They molded and cut this key from a silver spoon. One of them swallowed it before it could be found after they were captured."

"Good Lord." Severin put his hand to his throat.

"It unlocks the cells," Golden Eagle tried to hand the key to me, "but not the shackles. They knew they could not escape on their own. They had tried already, but they gave me the key to use when I was able to organize help."

"Give it to Severin." I pointed.

"I still do not fully…"

Severin snatched the key. "You get the dogs off us, we will get some tools to loose the chains."

"Hold it right there!" a voice from behind us ordered.

I hadn't been paying close enough attention. I thought the danger was with the dogs. Severin tucked the key in his watch pocket.

"Stand and turn slowly," the voice continued. "Any sudden or suspicious movements will be met with swift punishment. I assure you, I will worry with apologies later."

We raised our hands and turned around. There in the soft dark was the deputy sheriff and the man whose shotgun I had destroyed or the one I had hung from the tree.

"Get over here, both of you!"

Both? Golden Eagle had vanished.

"Thank goodness you found us!" Severin grabbed my arm and twisted it behind my back. "I found the Alabaster Kid for you."

"Shut it!" The men moved closer, still pointing their weapons. "I told you I'd worry about apologies later. Right now, Glenn here is going to tie *both* of your hands behind you."

As Glenn held a sight on us, the deputy pulled both of my pistols from the holsters and Severin's pistol from his vest and dropped them on the ground. Then he held point while Glenn tied our hands.

"This is ridiculous!" Severin protested as they marched us towards the growing sounds of the dogs. "I've been nothing but a help the whole time. Why, I'm just a simple artisan trying to make a buck…"

"Quiet!" Glenn ordered through a large white gauze wrapped around his jaw.

They prodded us into a ravine with dirt and roots sticking out above our heads. The moon had come out full, and even they could see around the shadows.

"Here." The deputy pushed us up against a crumbly clay wall.

Severin's feet slipped several times on the wet rocks at our feet.

TWEET! the deputy placed his fingers in his mouth and whistled long and piercing.

The dogs stopped barking for just the briefest of seconds before really kicking up a ruckus. They were soon right on top of us… literally. I looked up above us at the top of the ten-foot dirt cliff, only to have the soil thrown down into my face by the four jumping dogs pulling anxiously at the end of ropes. They were being barely contained by Sheriff Plummer. In the moonlight, even through his bushy mustache, I could see him smiling.

"Deputy Stone, you have done fine work tonight," he said. "We caught both of our quarry in one hunt."

"There's been a mistake." Severin struggled against the ropes.

"The mistake was not bringing you in sooner," the sheriff tied the dogs off to a small tree, "as soon as my men told me you were asking too many questions."

"I just wanted…"

"And the Alabaster Kid." The sheriff slid butt first down the side of the ravine. "WOOP! You *are* a slippery one! Good thing you two were together. The dogs only had Mr. Severin's scent to go on. They wouldn't follow yours."

"Dogs like me," I said.

"Don't you have somethin' to say to our Glenn here?" The sheriff opened his hand towards Glenn. "After all, you 'bout broke his jaw, and you laid his brother out somethin' fierce."

Glenn took a step forward.

"New gun?" I asked him.

"Yeah." He slammed the butt of his rifle into the side of my face. It knocked me to the ground. I decided to stay down and feign unconsciousness.

Glenn kicked me in the belly and again in the head. It was all I could do not to react. He kicked me in the belt and was about to kick me again when the deputy stopped him.

"All right, that's enough." The deputy grabbed his arm.

"The boy's jest lettin' off steam a little," the sheriff grunted. "'Sides, it won't matter much in a few minutes anyway."

I tensed to leap up and run, hoping it would give Severin the chance to run the other direction. Sheriff Plummer drew his gun.

"Now, hold on, Sheriff," Deputy Stone said. "We can give them a trial like the others and then put them away in the caves."

"Ya' cain't put everone in the caves, Stone." The sheriff bobbed his head. "You gonna babysit 'em?

"Perhaps they could be of benefit," Stone said. "Besides… they'll be missed."

"I got a idea." The sheriff walked over and put his arm around the deputy's shoulder. "We can lock them up until we get the Negros back inta' place. We'll have Mayor Hausman send out some telegraphs ta' buy us some time. Then we'll figure out some believable accidents for these fella's, you know, snake bites, rock slides. Heck, we can have a church beam fall down on our stained glass delivery man."

"I'm not much for murder in cold blood." Deputy Stone stepped away from the sheriff.

"Sure," the sheriff said. "They can be like that Ferrell boy when the Alabaster Kid shot him dead in the head."

"Good Lord!" Severin said, "You killed…"

"And you seen and heard too much, Severin." The sheriff turned. "There ain't no comin' back fer you."

"But what if I move here? What if I just stay in Veil and keep my mouth shut?" Severin said.

"You wouldn't fit in with our kind, Yank." The sheriff spat. "You can live here til you die, though."

The deputy turned to Glenn. "Bring him," he said. "I'll get Severin."

"No," the sheriff said. "Let Severin drag the bounty hunter government agent. It'll do him good to get a little exercise in the night air."

After a few minutes I "woke up" to save on Severin's endurance and my heels. Glenn constantly pushed us through nettles and vines until we came up to the entrance of the Spider Caves. Another man, one I had never seen before, was seated at the entrance. Not a single light burned in the interior and it was so dark, even I couldn't see inside.

CHAPTER FIFTEEN

Glenn lit a miner's torch and moaned as he strapped it on his head. The walls of the entrance were clay and dirt, much like the ravine we had been in earlier. As we were pushed in farther, the soil gave away to a yellow limestone that was filled with little holes. It was much like a frozen sponge. The occasional insect, spider, mouse, or centipede rolled out and then skittered from the light. The floor had been trampled down flat and hard by foot traffic. The deeper we got, probably only about twenty feet in, the rocks change to a harder stone. Severin started breathing quicker and had to be prodded by the deputy. I began to smell the distinct smell of humanity up ahead and after a few more steps, I could hear the shuffle of a crowd.

We came upon a rough wooden fence hewn into the rock wall. Behind it were a sea of eyes that only I could see. Men, women, children, even babies folded into the blackness of the cavern beyond. Their collective breathing made the entire area seem like a living thing, heaving in and out in a desperate rhythm. I could see people in rags and others in once fine clothes. All were filthy. In the dark, the dirt on their clothes made it look like holes in their bodies, like pieces of them were missing. Their eyes and mouths floated in the air. The things that made them more than shades, their very flesh was part of the dark. Slavery hadn't been abolished. It had just been moved to the shadows.

In less time than I had to ponder this aberration, I was herded to the right, down one of the spider's legs, past stores of grain and outcroppings of canned food and garbage and different kinds of refuse. We passed by an indentation where the three black men were. They were wearing farm clothes. Iron bars had been driven into the rock at the floor and ceiling. They stood as close to the bars as their ankle chains allowed. They had no shoes, and I saw no evidence of food or water. They all had their arms folded across their chest and their heads raised in defiance.

"Lincoln," I said in a hushed voice loud enough for one man to react by lowering his arms and jerking his head in my direction.

"Move it." Glenn gave me a firm push between my shoulder blades with the butt of his rifle.

There were a couple of men sitting in the back of the next cell. They were covered with old blankets and had their hats pulled down over their faces. They appeared to be asleep, but I could tell by their breathing that they weren't. They were not shackled to the wall.

"M'cold!" one man said. "I need another blanket."

"We'll bring ya' a couple more blankets later on," the sheriff spoke cheerfully behind us. "You can fight yer new bunk mates fer 'em."

Glenn grabbed me by the arm and pushed me into the cell past the rusty door.

"We'll come and get you for yore accidents," Glenn hissed.

"Come on boys," the sheriff took his own torch and walked off, "I got to feed the dogs. If things work out, we'll be gettin' our help back in a few days."

The deputy pushed Severin into the cell and closed the door. As Glenn turned to leave, Deputy Stone turned the key and locked us in. He put the key in his pocket. He stood there growing darker as Glenn walked away with the light. Once

Glenn rounded a bend, Deputy Stone stood there outside the cage in the total darkness.

"You have something to say?" Severin asked through the still air.

"He ain't got nothin' to say," one of the men behind us said. "He just likes to watch and take it all in."

After a moment, the deputy turned and walked off, dragging his hand along the cave wall to avoid falling.

"We need to…" Severin started.

I reached out and luckily grabbed his arm. Without any light at all, I could see nothing. There were times when I was a child when I would take all the books out of the large humpback chest and crawl inside. I felt the darkness comfort me. It told me that the answers were all out there; I just couldn't see them. The darkness would hold the answers for me until I could bring enough light to find them. When I could make myself bright enough, I would be able to find the answers to the mystery of myself.

This darkness was different though. I was not alone in this darkness, and I didn't trust the mysteries contained therein. Above the smell of human waste and spoiled food and clay and rock and dirt, there was something else. There was another familiarity.

"What brings you gentlemen to this predicament?" I said.

"We were just passin' through when we got wind of the little production they got goin' on here in Veil," one man said.

"I don't think it's just Veil," the other man said.

I heard them stand up.

"You cattlemen?" I asked.

"We've done some cattle," one man said. "We just come up to visit some fambly nearby."

They stepped towards me in unison. I pushed Severin back a few steps towards a side wall. I made sure to keep ahold of his arm.

"Yes," I said, "I met your cousin earlier today. Or is he your uncle?"

They stopped walking.

"Good Lord!" Severin jumped. "I stepped in a pile of mud… at least, I *hope* it's mud. Lord, let it be mud."

"Tell us!" One of the men ran forward a few steps. I could hear him flailing about, "Did the Indian trade work? We know who you are!"

"And I you," I said.

"Alabaster Kid!" the other man said. "Yore a dead man!"

"I'd save my threats for the man who killed your brother," I said. "Sheriff Plummer."

"Liar!" the man in front said.

"It's true," Severin spoke up. "I heard him say as much."

"Who the hell are you?" one of them said.

"Agent Arthur Severin of the United States Secret Service," Severin said.

"Harris is dead? OOF!" one man walked into the other.

"Well, he and Uncle Zakk ain't come fer us like they said," the other man said.

"Ty and Mission Ferrell," I said to Severin.

"So I gathered," he said.

"What happened to Zakk Griller?"

"I don't know," I said, "He got away."

"We can get you out of here," Severin said.

"I think not," I turned to Severin. "These men are criminals."

"These men are two extra men more than we had a few minutes ago," Severin took hold of my sleeve.

"I don't trust them," I said. "We can't trust them."

"Good thing," Ty said, "cause if we ever do get outa' here, I'm puttin' a bullet through those rags coverin' yer ugly face."

"Ty, you idiot." Mission hit Ty. "You don't *tell* them that. There'll be plenty of time to shoot them once we get outa' here."

"Point?" I asked.

"Point," Severin conceded.

"Uncle Zakk is still out there," one of them said. "He'll come get us, just like we helped bust him out."

A low hum came from down the tunnel out near the entrance to the main body of the spider. At first, even I could barely hear it. Ty and Mission squabbled and threatened. Severin pulled free and shuffled up to the bars. The hum became voices. The voices began to sing. The song filled the cave. The other three men in the cage between us and the main congregation joined together in the song. It was a sad hymn about freedom and salvation, a painful cry of redemption sung as only those who are captives can sing it.

"I was a slave to the wages of sin.
The world and the devil knew me,
but Jesus revealed a new life to begin.
Beneath the veil I was set free."

The Ferrells stumbled back to their cots and claimed them. They covered back up even though the moisture in the air permeated under all of our clothes. I stepped up closely behind Severin as the voices got louder. I tapped his watch pocket.

"Beneeeeeath the dark veil...
Beneath the dark veil I was free.
My Savior he saved me for eternity,
And beneath the dark veil I was free!"

"Take the key to them," I whispered. "Come right back."

Severin nodded. I began singing. I knew the chorus well even though I had never before heard it. It was a part of my soul.

"Oh, shut up!" one of the Ferrells moaned.

They never even noticed Severin slip from the cell using the homemade key. I kept singing loudly until I felt the door shift open to allow Severin back in. The singing of the captives helped not only to pass the time, but to build a brotherhood, a coalition with a single purpose.

"Now what?" Severin whispered. "They still have the shackles. They wouldn't…"

"Take off your shirt and stand in the mud," I said.

"Take off my…"

"Do it now before the silence starts again," I said.

They sang another verse and and another. I guided Severin over to where he had stood before. He pulled off the loose tie that had been dangling around his neck out of his collar and stuffed it into his pants pocket. He reluctantly handed me his vest and then his shirt. I handed him back his vest.

"Put it on," I said and pushed him farther into the mud pile until he was against the wall.

"Mmph!" Severin nearly stumbled. "I can't… This is as far…"

"Cup your hands and lift me on your shoulders," I placed his hands together.

When he had his fingers entwined, I put my muddy boot in his hands.

"OAFF!" Severin grunted as he lifted me up.

The singing continued.

"Don't look up," I said.

"What are they doing?" one of the Ferrells said.

One thing I noticed about the dirt was the smell. It was rich black topsoil. From what I could see outside, these caves were not deep. They were likely carved out of soft limestone from an underground stream. Some of them had already collapsed into gullies that had grown over in brush and small trees. I reached up to the ceiling and began digging. Dirt and rocks fell on my head and on Severin. We both spit. A large rock dislodged and started to fall. I was able to deflect it, although it nearly knocked Severin over.

"Watch it," I said after it had fallen.

Severin spit more dirt and debris. We both looked up into the starry night.

"Son of a…" Ty Ferrell said as he stood next to Mission.

With my long fingers and arms, I was able to pull myself up to freedom, but the loose rocks and soil threatened to collapse under me. I lay on my belly and handed down part of Severin's shirt.

"Grab on," I said.

As he did so, the Ferrells raced forward.

"Me next!" Mission cried.

"Damnation!" Severin swore. He kicked at them with his mud-crusted boots as I pulled him up.

The Ferrells grabbed his legs, and all three of them fell into the mud. The ground collapsed some more, and nearly sent me tumbling in.

"RRRAAAHHH!" an eerie scream erupted from me as I tried to right myself.

Severin stood, and I, halfway down the hole and hanging from my waist, grabbed the back of his vest and heaved. I pulled him out so fast that I flipped over and sent him rolling down the hill through a thicket.

The singing stopped abruptly. Almost immediately, the three men in the other cell began singing at the top of their lungs. The rest soon followed. I slid down the hill and found Severin lying on a rock, huffing and puffing.

"Good Lord, Kid," he said in between breaths. "We don't need those extra men."

"Call me Peter," I extended my dirty mud-encrusted hand, "Peter Tentman."

He took my hand and stood. I handed him his shirt.

"Where to now?" He took off his vest and put his shirt on.

"I think I know where the shackle keys are," I said.

"Well, now that we're out of this jailhouse," he buttoned his cuffs, "we can go get them. Where are they?"

"They're in the sheriff's jailhouse," I said. "We'll have to break in."

"Great."

"Don't worry," I looked through the woods. "I know someone who is very good at that."

CHAPTER SIXTEEN

You were supposed to free them, not just give them back the key." Golden Eagle sat in the shade of the large tree and smoked his pipe. "They already had the key once. You just gave it back to them."

"They needed more help than we could give at the time," Severin said. "If I can get word…"

"There were men in the main chamber as well as the small cell that were chained to the wall." I stood behind the tree and washed my face with some rags I had dipped in a stream. I dug some mud out from under the headband of my hat. I patted my guns that Golden Eagle had rescued after we were forced to drop them.

"You're sure Plummer has them?" Severin asked. "This shirt is ruined."

"I saw the large ring of keys when I brought Harris Ferrell in," I said. "I thought it queer that he would have so many keys for only two cells, and some were obviously for something else."

"You could have freed the prisoners in just the large room," Golden Eagle puffed. "Then in the chaos you wouldn't have to worry so much about the sheriff and his men hunting you down again. If I had been able to see what I was doing…"

"And how many would have died trying to escape?" I pulled and folded my wraps. "We need to get them ready to go as soon as we can get help here. Maybe we get some men on the high ground to give us cover. That's why you need to get those keys while I get a message out and the glass man goes for help."

"I'm not going anywhere." Severin sat next to Golden Eagle out of the sun. He cleaned the rim around his watch with a twig.

"One of us needs to get to the next town in case the message is stopped or redirected," I said. "This operation of theirs may spread all throughout the area."

"Think of another plan," Severin said. "Why would Plummer keep his keys in his office and not at the caves?"

"He doesn't trust anyone else," Golden Eagle said.

"Maybe." I finished wrapping my face. I slid the thin blade back under my wraps and turned my head in circles to make sure the blade was set comfortably. I put on my hat and sun cheaters and came back around to the other side of the tree. "I remember a man in the town I grew up in. He used to bring his own knives to the butcher shop. They were fine knives but not even as good as Mr. Crenshaw's. He insisted that Mr. Crenshaw use only the knives the man brought in. He was sure his knives were the best in town, even better than Crenshaw the butcher's." I sat beside Golden Eagle. He offered me his pipe, but I put up my hand.

"Bad form," he said and offered the pipe again.

I took a few puffs and coughed until my glasses fell off. Golden Eagle chuckled and handed the pipe to Severin who puffed away like it was mist off a morning pond.

"Anyway… AKK… SSssss…" a rattle and a hiss escaped from deep in my throat. I sat up straight and looked at them both in embarrassment.

They acted like they didn't notice.

"The man had to watch Mr. Crenshaw's every move," I said, "clicking and humming his disapproval with every cut. When Mr. Crenshaw was done, the man always found excuses to undercut the price by ten percent."

"What has this got to do with our plan?" Severin said.

"What did your teacher, Mr. Crenshaw do about this man?" Golden Eagle placed a small square of hardened leather over most of the bowl on his pipe. He drew breath several times until the tobacco glowed bright red and yellow. "I would have told the man to take his business elsewhere."

"It didn't seem to bother Mr. Crenshaw much." I shrugged. "He just made sure to always raise the initial price twenty percent."

"Ha!" Severin stuck a blade of grass in his mouth.

"Still, his reputation was damaged," Golden Eagle said.

"Everybody knew Billy Crenshaw's honor," I said. "This man couldn't hurt it."

"My uncle once cut off a buffalo's head using only stone tools." Golden Eagle offered the pipe to me once again.

"Please no," I said.

"Very well." He smiled. "He had a perfectly good set of knives too, but I can still see him in the blood and the mud, hacking away at that poor dead beast."

"What would make a man do that?" Severin said.

"He tied the head on a hedge tree until the buzzards got to it." Golden Eagle looked off in to the distance. "My brothers and I called it the buffalo tree for many years, even after my uncle's death."

"My parents made my brother wear a dress until he started school," Severin said.

Golden Eagle and I looked at him.

"My only concern is in getting my own people back," Golden Eagle said. "I am not overly concerned with the others."

"You have made that clear," I said.

"It is not my fight."

"I thought we were just telling childhood stories," Severin said. "I mean, it wasn't like I had to wear the dress. It was my brother..."

"I am surprised that your main concern is not capturing your bounty." Golden Eagle puffed at the dying pipe.

"My main concern is never just catching the criminal," I said.

"Yes," Golden Eagle looked at his pipe bowl, "that is why I follow your plan."

"I mean, what was the purpose...?" Severin said.

"The sheriff operates out of pride and showmanship." I looked around for something to get the taste of the pipe out of my mouth. "He has to hold the keys. He has to run the dogs. He has to be in control."

"Not so." Golden Eagle picked in his pipe with the pointed end of a small well-used chicken bone. "He operates out of fear. He must hold the reins to prevent a stampede."

"That would explain the mayor," Severin said. "He seems to be a nice enough man, if timid, but I got the distinct impression that Plummer pulls the strings in Veil."

"Perhaps the sheriff thinks you have fled." Golden Eagle tapped his spent tobacco out on the edge of one of the tin plates we had used for breakfast.

"I doubt it," Severin tossed the chewed grass away.

"I don't think so." I took a swig of cold coffee and winced. It was almost as bad as the pipe.

"Once they are all free," Golden Eagle said, "I will take my people to safety."

"We need you to help keep them all safe," I said. "There are dozens of them."

"They can help keep themselves safe." He placed his pipe in a small black satchel. "Will they not fight for their own freedom?"

"They're not soldiers," Severin said. "Part of our job is to fight for them."

"Every man is a warrior who is not free." Golden Eagle's face grew cold. The lines became clearer, and he clenched his jaw. "No matter the color, you see what happens to them when they cow to another."

"Why haven't we heard from your men, then?" Severin narrowed his eyes. "Why haven't we had an insurrection from the braves on the inside?"

"The three men in the other cell tried," I said.

"I would not expect it from my people." Golden Eagle's upper lip twitched once as he looked down at the plates. "One of them is my elderly aunt. The other is my nine-year-old daughter, who we have been calling Mary."

We sat quietly in the cool fall breeze. It swelled and died.

"Well, I wouldn't expect..." Severin turned and stood. He stepped into the sun towards the horses.

"We are the only ones left of our family." Golden Eagle also stood. "Influenza ravaged our home, or what was left of it after the most of us were consigned to a reservation when I was a boy. I escaped, as did a few others, for what good it did. This land is no longer free to all."

"In any case," I said, "it would take several days for help to arrive, even assuming that the nearby towns aren't en-meshed in this practice as deeply as Veil, and since neither of you is willing to follow my plan, we'll have to come up with something better."

"We cut off the head of the serpent," Golden Eagle said.

"Meaning?" I stood.

"We can't just shoot Plummer." Severin walked back up to the tree. "I'm not going to just start shooting people. My initial assignment was just to observe and report back."

"I am not leaving my family in that hole while we wait for your government to decide what to do to them." Golden Eagle gathered the plates and cups.

"They're too spread out," I said. "There are men in town, men at the caves, possibly in surrounding farms."

"If we remove the sheriff, the rest will fall in line." Golden Eagle tied the plates and cups into a leather bag and placed it in the crook of the tree we were under.

"We don't know that," Severin said. "What if they kill the slaves? What if they decide to destroy the evidence before we can get some federal marshals in here? What about your family?"

"You dare?" Golden Eagle grabbed Severin by the shirt. "I tell you about my family, and you use them to manipulate me?"

"Whoa!" Severin raised his hands.

"I should do this myself!" Golden Eagle pushed Severin away. "I should never have gotten involved with you white men. My family would be free by now. I would find a way."

"I'm getting tired of being compared to all these 'white men' you talk about." Severin straightened his shirt. "I spend my life trying to help people, no matter what color they are."

"And I'm not exactly white, although it may be hard to tell," I walked in between the two men, "at least as far as I know."

"You help people." Golden Eagle turned his back on us and began to walk away. "Just how many people have you helped that weren't white?"

Severin watched him walk away. He turned his eyes towards me. "Well, I'm trying to help some right now," he said. "We just don't have enough people."

"We need to send a telegraph," I said. "Though I imagine someone will be guarding the station."

Severin rubbed the stubble on his cheeks. "I may know where we can get some allies."

"Here in Veil?"

"And a quick shave too," Severin said, "I wager."

CHAPTER SEVENTEEN

"We had squirrel jerky for breakfast," Severin wiped his clean shaven face with his handkerchief, "and boiled greens, I think." He tugged and tightened his now tattered tie.

"I have pickled squirrel." Mother Fellows set the muffins on the small round table with the tatted doily.

"Had." I said as I scooped some butter from a small gray crock. "There were three jars in the cellar."

"How do you pickle a squirrel?" Golden Eagle sat apart from us in the sitting room on a small ornate loveseat.

"The same way you pickle all your small game." Mother Fellows handed a fresh muffin to Severin and myself. "Not that I'd expect you to know anything about the finer points of proper food preparation. If it ain't burnt over a fire in the woods, yore kind don't know squat about it."

"Tell me again why I agreed to come here with you?" Golden Eagle said. "This back woods old woman…"

"I simply meant that as a man you have jest the basic understanding of what we women folk go through." She wiped her hands on her apron. "Cherish, go tell Uncle Zakk that his visitors will receive him proper now."

The preteen girl had been hiding behind the doorframe to the entrance hall, occasionally peeking in on the strangers. She remained silent, but slipped away to do her grandmother's bidding.

"Would you say she's about nine?" Severin looked over his muffin towards Golden Eagle.

"Three months ago." Mother Fellows set a plate and a cup between Severin and me. "She is a deep thinkin' child. She hardly marries two sentences together, but then she comes out with the mostest wisest things."

I heard a gun cock as Griller made his way down the stairs. I had my hand on mine in a second, and Severin was reaching for his.

"Not in my house!" Mother Fellows demanded. "Not again. Not if'n I have any say about it."

Griller entered the room, grumbling. He used his gun to tuck his shirt in over his large belly into his low riding black pants.

"Yore just lucky there's a lady present," he said.

"No, you are lucky I don't take you in right here." I kept my hand on my gun.

"No, YORE lucky I don't…"

"Alright, yore both lucky!" Mother Fellows waved her fingers between us. "Now hesh!"

""Fresh biscuits," Griller mumbled some more and reached between us to the table, scowling the whole way. "And yore the lucky one."

"Muffins!" Mother Fellows took the tray to the fireplace mantle. "Sit down. These men have agreed to talk civil and you will too."

"What do I want with some ungodly freak and some federal law man?" Griller plopped down in the small chair between us. It squeaked in protest.

"You said you'd talk," Mother said.

"We need more guns to take control of this town," I leaned forward. "We plan on taking out the sheriff."

"NOT killing him," Severin interjected.

"We'll keep him and his men locked up in the cells at Spider Cave until federal marshals can get here." I played with the tatting on the table.

Griller grabbed up the remaining muffins and began stuffing them in his mouth. I pushed the crock of butter towards him.

"What's in it fer me?" he asked between bites. "You know what I want."

"I can't grant you clemency," Severin said, "and we don't even have the time to notify the proper authorities."

"Well, we will," I said, "but they won't get here in time, I expect."

"I want to walk," he said, "or I walk."

"We can do that," Severin said. "In all the confusion, people won't notice…"

"What?" I pulled the crock back. "We most certainly can NOT let this man go!"

"Muzzle yore dog, law man, or we got no deal." Griller wiped his mouth on his sleeve.

"Everyone wants to commit evil with impunity." I bunched up my fist on the table. "The wages of sin, may I remind you…"

"You owe me, Alabaster Kid." Mother Fellows stood over me. "I gave you sanctuary. I never even told my own kin, who would surely a' done you harm."

"Yer dang lucky," Griller said under his breath.

"I took you into my home, fed you, nursed, you." She swooped her arms around. "You would take my servants from me and cause my home to fall into ruin, yet I helped you."

"And just why did you do that?" I turned in my chair. "I have a difficult time believing it was all because you thought I could save you from the law. You know good and well I don't have that power. So why was it, Mother Fellows? What made you help out a freak like me?"

Mother Fellows looked across the room to the young girl hiding by the doorframe. "I have my reasons," she said in a voice suddenly docile. "This family ain't all sinners. They's hope fer some of us yet."

"Mother Fellows," I said, "this man…"

"I know perfectly well about this man," she snipped. "I will not have you stirring up his dishonor while his niece is in the other room."

"A brief respite, then." I looked over to Cherish and pushed the crock of butter back to Griller. "That is all I can promise. I will find him again, and so will justice."

"Oh, justice my foot," she said.

"How can the three of us take the whole blamed town?" Griller scooped up a chunk of butter using a half-eaten muffin.

"Four of us," I looked over to Golden Eagle and Severin pointed.

"God," Griller shook his head. "Worst gang I ever been in. All this fer a pile a' darkies."

"I could slit his throat right now and be rid of him." Golden Eagle leaned forward. A stern look from Mother Fellows led him to slowly sit back up in silence.

"I don't ever count the injuns," Griller took a long drink of his coffee, "not even the ones I killed."

Golden Eagle visibly shook. He stood with as much composure as he could muster and walked through into the front room. He opened the door and stepped out with his rifle.

"You can't expect…" I said.

Gunshots erupted from the porch.

"Good Lord!" Severin jumped up. "He'll attract the sheriff!"

In one movement, I was up and out of the room. Griller choked on his coffee. Mother Fellows put her hands to her mouth. I was met at the door by Golden Eagle rushing back in.

"Gunmen!" he shouted. "At the edge of the woods!"

CHAPTER EIGHTEEN

"We got the sheriff and the whole posse out here, red man," a voice came from the woods.

"We got the whole place surrounded!" another voice hollered.

"You come out with yore hands up," the first voice said, "and no injun tricks, you hear?"

"I don't hear or see any horses." I opened the window in the sitting room a crack.

"There's nobody out back." Severin came in through the hallway. "That I can tell, anyway."

"I only saw one of them," Golden Eagle said, "as he ducked behind a tree. They fired wild. I'm not even sure they hit the house."

"Lord, I hope not." Mother Fellows came out of the cellar and closed the door behind her. "There's been enough damage to this house lately as it is."

She intentionally straightened the heavy drapes over the boarded window I had jumped through. She looked pointedly in my direction. "Do you know how difficult this is gonna be ta' fix without my servants?"

"You do know that if you keep people against their will and make them work for you for free, they're not really servants." I walked into the front room.

"I feed 'em and clothe 'em and house 'em." She put her hands on her hips. "It's a lot better'n what they get out on their own."

"So they owe you," I said sarcastically. I opened the door a crack. "Yes, I'm familiar with your methods."

Griller pulled back the curtain on the large window on the other side of the door.

"If I c'n jest get a clean shot." He pulled his gun up to his head and reared back.

"You bust that window, I bust yore head!" Mother Fellows took ahold of his ear and drug him away from the window.

"Ow, ow, Mother, dang it!" Griller stood and pushed her hand away, "This is serious."

"Quiet down." I waved my hand at them. "I can hear them arguing."

"I don't hear nothin'," Griller said.

"Griller," I flung the door open. "Get out there."

"What in tarnation you at about, boy?" Griller stood behind Mother Fellows.

"Go get your stupid kin," I said.

"Mah kin?"

"There's no sheriff or posse out there," I said. "It's your two nephews, Mission and Ty."

CHAPTER NINETEEN

"It's the only reason I agreed ta' work with 'em," Griller told the two filthy men sitting on an old wooden bench at the foot of the stairs. "That sheriff done shot yore brother dead."

"I say let's go git him ourselves," Ty said. "We don't need their help."

"Oh, the bullet'll be ours, boys," Griller patted up dust on Ty's shoulder, "but it's better to have multiple targets."

"Glad your priorities are straight," Severin frowned.

"I ain't got no love fer that alabaster freak," Griller pointed at me. "I still cain't sleep at night fer him twistin' my spine in our dustup."

"It's your own fault," I said. "I didn't make you rob that store or shoot that man or his horse."

"That weren't me, no how." Griller spit as he spoke. "That was all Lenny Fish what done the shootin'."

"That's enough." Severin stepped in between us. "Get it together."

"He's jest dang lucky that we all need each other right now, is all," Griller said.

"No, *you* are just lucky that I don't take you out and go on without you," I said.

"Let me tell you who's lucky." Griller pushed past Severin and got in my face.

"Oh, good Lord!" Severin pushed us apart. "If we're even half as lucky as you two keep shouting, we won't have any problem at all."

"Well, we got us a gang now." Griller spit on the floor. "What're we awaitin' fer?"

"I want to try to get to the telegraph station and send for help," I said. "We can lay low a couple more days here at Mother's…"

"If we can keep from killing each other." Severin looked between me and Griller.

"This ain't good fer the girl," Mother said, "but I don't suppose there's no other choice."

"It is not good for any of the girls," Golden Eagle said from the other room, "not here, not in those caves. If you had listened to me…" He walked through the doorway.

"Those men refused!" Severin walked over to Golden Eagle. "Lincoln, Jed, Everett, they refused to leave without everyone else."

"What do you mean?" I said.

"When they escaped before, the others in the large room wouldn't go without the men who were chained to the wall," Severin dug around in his pants pocket, "Lincoln said they all agreed to stay, everyone to a person. Everyone, Golden Eagle, refused to leave without the others. Look! Here's the key they made. They wouldn't take it."

He handed the key to me. Golden Eagle turned and spoke in his native language under his breath. I didn't know what he said, but it was sad. It had a weight to it that had been borne too long. He turned and went back into the sitting room. He sat on the loveseat and stared at the fireplace on the opposite wall.

"I can run a telegraph machine," Severin said. "I'll go send a message to Washington. They can contact the proper authorities."

"We already know that there's a spy in your office," I said. "I know how to operate a telegraph too, but who do you think would have a better chance of getting there?"

"I can manage just fine."

"At night."

Severin looked at me in silence.

"Golden Eagle can get the keys from the sheriff's office at the same time," I said.

"We will need a diversion," Severin said. "Perhaps Griller and the boys…"

"Fire," Golden Eagle stood and walked to the fireplace. "Catch the whole cursed town up in walls of fire."

"That's not exactly what I had in mind," Severin said, "although it might work."

"We are not setting the town on fire," I said. "It could kill innocent people."

"None of these people are innocent," Golden Eagle said.

"Be that as it may…"

"I know a building we can sacrifice," Severin put his hands behind his back, "a building that is set apart from the rest, a building that is supposed to be all about sacrifice, but has come to be used as a symbol of opulence and privilege."

"The church." Mother Fellows stepped up. "Heaven help us, you wanna burn the church."

"We can't burn a church," I said. "That's sacrilege."

"It hasn't been consecrated yet," Severin said to both of us. "It isn't even built. Besides, the church isn't a building. We're all taught that in school."

"We can find…" I stopped. Something caught my ear. "One horse," I said.

"What?" Severin looked out the window with Griller.

"I don't hear nothin'," Mission said.

"There's a horse coming," I said. "Get to the cellar."

"No!" Mother Fellows put her hand on my chest, "Cherish is still in there from the scare a few minutes ago. Y'all head upstairs. I'll take care a' whoever it is."

"Head to the extra bedroom," Griller led the way. "I got ammo that'll work fer most a' you."

We went up the wide staircase. I stayed to the rear. As they all went inside the spare room, I hugged the hall wall to listen in on the conversation.

"Keep them from doing anything stupid," I whispered to Severin as he entered the bedroom, "and keep Golden Eagle from killing them all for doing something stupid."

"Right."

I heard boots on the front porch. Then the front door opened and a man stepped inside without any knock or introduction.

"Mother Fellows." He left the front door open like he was in a hurry.

"Why, deputy," there was a smile in her voice, "I hope you brought news that the nice man who delivered the church glass will have enough left over ta' fix my front winda'."

"No, ma'am," he said, "I just want to inform you that the sheriff has called a town meeting for seven o'clock tonight. He wants all the residents to be there."

Some oaf in the bedroom stepped on a squeaky floorboard. The sound seemed to be magnified in its ill timing. The deputy and Mother Fellows heard it too. Neither of them spoke for a moment.

"Would you like a piece of pie?" Mother Fellows finally said.

"Is there someone up there?" The deputy took a step towards the stairs. His boots tread heavily on the old wood floor.

"It's jest Cherish," Mother Fellows said. "You know what a quiet child she is."

The deputy stood for a moment and listened. I caught myself holding my breath.

He walked towards the front doorway and placed his hand on the heavy oak door. The hinges cried softly as he closed the door and latched it with himself still inside the house.

"Who is upstairs, Mother?"

"I told you," Mother Fellows' voice quivered, "Cherish is jest…"

"Cherish is standing right there by the cellar door," the deputy said in a calm measured tone.

He walked up to the first step and placed his boot on it. I placed my left hand on my Colt.

"I told you, there's no one there," Mother turned and grabbed his arm. "Deputy, please!"

Deputy Stone took another step. He pulled his gun from his holster.

"Who's upstairs, Mother?" he asked again.

The old woman stepped lively up to him and once again took his arm.

"Jason," her voice was pleading, "I implore you. There is… nobody up those stairs."

"Mother."

"Do you remember the piana' I had in the dining room when you was a child?" she pulled down on his gun arm.

"Now is not…"

"I used ta' play it fer you and Kathy and those Smith boys," she said. "Remember?"

"I remember."

"Remember when yore daddy wanted ta' send you off to that fancy school?" she asked. "Remember how proud he was a' you?"

The deputy didn't speak.

"Why, he didn't have enough copper ta' mend a sow's ear, let alone send his gifted son to the city fer some proper learnin'." Her voice grew sad. "You ever wonder what happened ta' that old piana', 'er how yore daddy was able ta' get you ta' Kansas City on a dirt farmer's salary?"

"Sometimes he was a fool who dreamed too big," Deputy Jason Stone said in a hush.

"And sometimes he knew when it was important ta' listen to yore heart," Mother Fellows said. "Listen to yore heart, Jason Stone. There ain't nobody at the top of them stairs."

Deputy Stone stood on those stairs. I could see his shadow searching for me, reaching for me. After a time, he walked back to the door and opened it.

"You always did like taking in strays, Mother Fellows," he said.

"And you was one, deputy," Mother Fellows said. "You was one."

"Seven o'clock," he said from the porch. "I'll understand if you aren't there. I'll stop by after the meeting for that piece of pie. Maybe you can show me the greens you have put up for winter. We'll reminisce again… about the old days when this town was closer and we could trust our neighbors."

Severin opened the door and looked out at me as the deputy rode away. Mother Fellows wept at the foot of the stairs.

"We just ran out of time," I said.

CHAPTER TWENTY

I could already smell the fire on the wind. It hadn't even been discovered yet, and I could sense it. It wouldn't take long now that the sun was fully down to see the flames, even from the town hall meeting up the road. I was outside of town on New Moon. I was heading out to the telegraph station to send for help. There was no way it would actually get there in time to help us, but the authorities would know what was going on and maybe be able to either justify or avenge us. By the time I reached the station hill, I could see the lights above the town caused by the dancing flames.

"I understand your pain." The little mayor who I had spoken to before at the station walked around the darkened building. His name was Ned Hausman. Severin told me he was not just the mayor and the telegraph engineer, but the postmaster and fire chief as well. "Still," he said, "you shouldn't go around setting fires. It's not natural."

"There is nothing more natural than fire," I said, "or more ancient."

He was wiping down a strange short nosed pistol, the likes of which I had never seen before. With a slow casual brush, I let my hand slide down towards my gun, but he must have been able to see better than I thought. He raised his pistol at me.

"You can't use this station," he said in a practiced tone. "It's closed for business."

"What did you…"

"*You* busted it up with a wooden club," Hausman petted his gun, "at least, that is what I will tell the sheriff when he gets here."

"I can shoot you before you can even pull the trigger," I spoke calmly but with authority. "You know I can."

There was fear in his eyes, yet there was a casualness about his voice. He didn't seem like he was overly confident, more like he didn't really care what happened.

"Maybe," he shrugged. "I'm not a gunfighter. I'm really not much of any kind of fighter. Perhaps that is why the sheriff appointed me to so many plum positions in town."

"I'm going into that building." I slipped down off New Moon. "Please. I don't want to hurt you."

"This gun is evil, and so is anyone who uses it." Hausman pointed his pistol straight up, "Imagine... *me* as the fire chief. Some joke, yes?"

He pulled the trigger, and fire shot into the night sky. A blinding flash lit up the countryside all around as the payload exploded.

"This...this is the first time it has done some good," Hausman let out a squeak and dropped the weapon in the dirt, "and the first time it has been fired since the accident that killed my wife and daughter. Funny how it survived the flames."

He fell to his knees and wept openly.

"The sheriff... the sheriff will be here shortly," he sniffed. "There was no meeting. It was all a ploy to draw you out."

I walked over to the unlocked door and turned the handle.

"You been to Briar Town or Chum?" Hausman remained on his knees and hung his head as he spoke.

"No."

"They have agents working with Sheriff Plummer. They find and capture and trade the Negros," he said. "I couldn't let the sheriff contact them. I was supposed to have sent a message days ago. He will probably kill me when he finds out."

I stood over him. My shadow cast a blue darkness on his huddled form. "You knew that Severin was the agent," I said, "and you never said anything."

"What was that boy thinking?" Hausman said. "He had it all. He made it out, but he was never the same after Melinda... after my daughter..."

"Todd Plummer."

"This isn't right. I notified the people I trust at Fort Bright. They will be here as soon as possible, but it may be too late." He looked out over the town. "The sheriff will be here soon. You need to leave. This flare will give you time. He'll be looking for you here, but you won't be here."

"Come with me," I said.

"I'm not a fighter," his knees cracked and popped as he stood, "I'm more of the coward type."

"Not from where I'm standing," I said.

"Perhaps if I hadn't spent so many years playing along, I could see your point, but seeing you brought it all back. Seeing what the sheriff was capable of drove it home," he said. "I'll lead him around in circles for a while until he catches on. You go on. He probably has twenty men with him by now."

I mounted New Moon and headed back down the hill the other way. I had little doubt that Golden Eagle was able to get the keys, but there was bound to be a heavy guard at the caves.

On the way down, I passed the deputy and two other men, the butcher and the blacksmith. I saw them early enough to send New Moon over the hill and to hide myself in the brush. There was no sheriff and no dogs. Either he was at the fire or the jailhouse or the caves.

I led New Moon through the shadows behind the buildings in town. The church fire was being attended poorly by the town's women and a couple of old men and a child or two.

This was not a chore for which they were trained. It appeared that Hausman was not lying. The men of Veil were out searching for us.

I headed out to our meeting spot, praying that the others would be waiting.

CHAPTER TWENTY-ONE

"You look terrible." I knelt down in our regular meeting spot outside the Spider Cave entrance in the patch of 'itchy' weeds whose small nettles were just enough of an irritant to keep the animals from trampling them. "What happened?"

"I was introduced to an unfriendly fist." Severin patted his nose with the remains of his handkerchief. "I gagged him with my tie and tethered him to a tree with my reins, but it's just a matter of time before he alerts all the others."

"It's not like they're not expecting us," I said. "Hopefully the mayor is taking some of them the long way back."

"The mayor?"

"Plague of conscience." I peered through the tall weeds. "Or God has softened his heart."

Four men paced the entrance of the cave. There were others in the woods all around us. Even if they didn't see or hear us, it was just a matter of time before they just accidentally bumped right into us.

"Golden Eagle…" Severin whispered.

I stopped him by putting my finger up to his mouth and my hand in front of his face. There were footfalls and the sound of swishing leaves nearby. The steps came closer, stopped, and then continued in another direction. I put my hands down.

"Golden Eagle is already inside," Severin whispered on breath that quivered in its softness. "At least I think he is. He was here, then he was gone. He got the keys from the sheriff's office just in time. The sheriff actually came back to get them while he was in the office."

"How on earth did he…?"

"You got me." Severin hunched down even more. "That is one skill I definitely need to learn, but now there's no doubt Plummer knows we are out here somewhere and we're headed to the caves."

"The Ferrells?" I asked. "And Griller?"

"The boys said there are some large round rocks up on top of the hill," Severin pointed, "like that big dark one there by the mouth of the cave."

"Yes," I said, "I saw them when we escaped."

"Well, they got out by sunrise and saw them too," Severin shifted his weight, "They're taking point up top to cover us getting in and out once we get the signal."

"I'm not looking for a massacre," I said. "On either side."

"I'm not either, but I'm not especially worried about their side," Severin said. "If it'll help, I imagine the odds are heavily in their favor."

"That's very helpful," I said. "Thank you."

"Once we're back out with the slaves, we'll have cover up top and those big red rocks down below, as well as the trees and the night." Severin looked up at the stars. "There's that crossing we took at the river. It's small, but that just means it's harder for them to find."

"When we cross that river, we'll have to scatter." I tightened a knot in my wrappings and pulled my gloves up. "Except for me. I'll stand point and hold them off as long as I can."

"I'm the federal agent," he said. "If anyone…"

There was a scuffle up ahead. I could see up atop the hill over the cave, one of the Ferrells was wrestling with another man.

"We don't have time to wait for Golden Eagle to free those men," I said. "He'll have to do it under fire."

I started to stand, but knelt down once again as Ty Ferrell was tossed off the hill. He landed hard on his back. The wind was knocked out of him, and he lay on the ground trying to roll over, trying to breathe. Four guns on the ground below were trained on him until he was able to catch his breath and sit up. They jerked him to his feet, and he used his newly caught breath to curse and threaten. I raised my pistol.

"Don't," hissed Severin. "You'll give up our position. Plus you could miss and hit Ferrell."

"I can do it," I said. "I can see better than you."

"But you can't shoot better than me," he said. "I know. I've seen it and so has Harris Ferrell. You're good, but you're not perfect. You might hit one of the other men."

I lowered my gun.

"They will probably just…" Severin said.

""Let him go!" the sheriff's voice amplified from the cave. "Let him go. We got way too many men here for anybody ta' get past us. We got his guns, and we done filled up the cell with alla' the male slaves and even one feisty injun."

"They got…"

"Ya' hear that, Agent?" The sheriff stood at the edge of the black wall of shadow inside the mouth of the cave. "We got yer injun!"

I raised my gun again.

"Are you crazy?" Severin put his hand on my Colt. "There are innocent people in that cave, women and children. You don't want a bullet ricochetting around in there."

I tensed my jaw and lowered my gun. A sound like a rattlesnake slithered up from my throat. Severin pulled back.

"The Lord would guide my bullets," I said.

"Did He guide the one that creased your back?" Severin leaned back up into my face. "He sure as hell didn't guide the

106

one that killed my father. God doesn't guide bullets, He condemns them."

The stars glowed in his eyes as he stared me down.

The men at the cave pushed Ty away from them. He stumbled a few steps and then began to run.

BANG!

A shot rang out from the cave entrance. Ty collapsed in the grass, dead. The sheriff walked out into the light. His gun was still smoking.

"Okay, now!" Severin said.

We both raised our guns, but another fired first. All the men scattered for cover. The sheriff ducked back into the darkness as three more shots fired. The body of a large man, the one who had been wrestling Ty, fell from above the caves. He writhed in agony as the damage from a bullet in his chest did its evil work. For a moment after he died, there was silence. Then the men below started firing blindly up the hill, rapidly at first, then more measured to conserve on ammunition.

""They've got the front too well guarded," Severin said. "No one can get in there."

"Good," I said.

"And now they've got Golden Eagle locked away with a dozen other men."

"Even better," I said.

"Why's that?"

"That means he's still alive," I began to work my way out of the weeds, "and with most of the men concentrated at the cave, there are less out looking for us. Let's go."

"Go where?" Severin followed.

"Spider Cave," I said. "I know a way in."

CHAPTER TWENTY-TWO

"There are times when rocks are better than a gun," I said.

"Yes, I know," Severin walked up behind me, "unless you fractured his skull."

"He's alive." I looked down at the melon-sized brown stone in my hand. "I can hear him breathing."

"For now," Severin said.

"You have a better idea?" I dropped the stone to the ground.

He paused and looked down the hill behind us. He could still easily see the man a few feet below us, and he could possibly see the man a little farther down who was tied and gagged with the extra bandages I brought. I doubt he could see the man at the base of the hill that we ambushed, and I pistol whipped into unconsciousness. I could still see him, but I wasn't sure I could still see him breathing.

"It's quieter than a gun." Severin puffed as we climbed up the hill that led to the top of the caves, to the section over the cell we were captives in just the day before. "You got the tie-up-and-gag idea from me, didn't you."

"You think I never had to tie up and gag a man before?" I asked.

I found the hole we had climbed out of the day before, and I started crawling into it.

"I hope they didn't relock the cell," Severin said, "otherwise this brilliant plan of yours is not so very."

"I have the spoon key," I said and dropped down into the rocks and soft mud below. "Remember?"

There was enough starlight that I could just make out the bars. No one else was in the cell as far as I could tell. Severin fell down in behind me. I took him by the elbow and led him to the cell door.

"Unlocked." I swung the door open.

The squeak of the hinges that had been so alarming earlier was now muted by the ringing of occasional gunfire. I noted that the rapidity of the shots was reduced. Ammo was probably running low. Griller brought as much as they could easily carry, so my hope was that they were still fine. It was strange indeed to be hoping that Griller and Ferrell were fine and well stocked with bullets. Early on, I feared that they might turn and run, but since Ty was killed, they were now fighting for vengeance.

As I started feeling my way down the corridor, I got something I needed. There was a small ball of orange light up ahead, helping guide me down the tunnel. As I approached the source, it was obvious who and what it was.

"Golden Eagle," I walked up to the second cell, "I never thought I would be glad to see and smell that awful pipe."

He was pressed up against the bars. Behind him were probably a dozen men. I could barely see their faces in the impossibly dim light. With my eyes though, that light was all that I needed to see what I wanted. I rifled through my pocket for the key.

"We must free the children," one man whispered.

"Help us," a voice came from the back.

"Have you seen my family?" Golden Eagle asked.

"I haven't been in the big room yet." I fiddled with the flimsy key. "Hold your pipe lower so I can see the lock mechanism better."

The men shuffled and pushed to let Golden Eagle lower the pipe. I placed the key and felt for the tumblers.

"I could strike a…"

Everything was instantly white as something struck me from the side. My head was on fire with pain and my ears sounded as if my head was a clapper in a church bell. The darkness poured back in as Golden Eagle struck a match. A man with a spade bore down on me with a determined ferocity. I spun but was still caught above the elbow by the blade.

"RrruuhHH!" Severin tackled the man and threw him into the bars. The shovel clanged against the metal.

Each sound reverberated in my head. There was an echo and a dull throb. I shook my head to clear it, but that only brought out more pain. I held my shaking hand up to the side of my head and tried to shut it all out. My blood was pumping loudly in my ears, drowning out the other sounds. I got up on one knee. The air in the tunnel seemed to push back down on me.

The man pushed Severin back into the darkness and Golden Eagle had to drop the match. I stood and shook my head again, disregarding the pain. The shovel whizzed by my head again in the darkness. It caused me to jump backwards into the stone wall behind me. I heard the clanging on the bars once again, and a man fell on me in the dark. I grabbed him by the collar and drew back to strike with all my might.

"It's me!" Severin said.

I tossed him aside just as the man swung his shovel again. It hit me in my right shoulder, but did little damage. My hands shot out like I was drawing my weapon. I caught the shovel at the handle just below the blade. I jerked it from his hands as the cell door flew open. The men poured out on top of us. They began striking and pulling and tearing like a single wild beast.

"It's me!" I echoed Severin's cry between blows.

Golden Eagle lit another match, and Severin began pulling men back.

"Get off him!" he shouted. "Get off!"

The men pulled back and calmed themselves.

"That was bound to alert someone." Severin took the gun from the now unconscious man's holster. "Can't tell if there's any bullets, but we need to go."

He handed the gun to a man behind him. Lincoln picked up the shovel. "We will be free," he said.

I took off my colts and handed them off as well.

"You must keep a weapon," one of the men said.

"I'll be fine," I said, "Go!"

I pulled my knife out of its hiding place at my neck. I wasn't sure, but it might have been slightly dented by a glancing blow from any of a hundred different things in the past few days. I handed it to Golden Eagle who was now on his next match.

"You give me your only weapon?" He took the blade with hesitation. "I will use it well. We must free all the others, and I am almost out of matches."

As he passed by, another man involuntarily recoiled as the light revealed my face. The spade had torn some of the rags and allowed others to fall away.

"I am with you all." I stepped back into the darkness. "Now, go!"

As we approached the large room, I could start to see somewhat better. The starlight lit up a small patch by the entrance, but I could see deeper into the room than anyone else. The blackness was more of a dark blue that revealed the true darkness hidden within.

Several of the sheriff's men entered the room and were met by the men I had just freed. I kicked the wooden gate down. My strength was renewed by the battle. A deluge of women and children joined the fray. I saw Golden Eagle put his arms around a woman and a little girl. The fight spilled out into the night, and they slipped into it as well. A couple of children whimpered in the back corner where I couldn't see.

"Just a little more light," I said. "I need just a little more light."

Like an answered prayer, the entire cavern lit up in a dancing yellow light. I could see the children in the dirt, holding each other. They were sickly and crying. I spun to see a man with a torch at the mouth of the cave.

"Din't see you in the crush." Glenn stood there with a torch in one hand and a rifle in the other. "Figured you'd still be inside.

"You fool!" I hissed. "You'll kill us all, shooting that thing off in here."

"Worth the gamble." He cocked the rifle, single-handedly. "I don't figure on missing, so I won't hafta' worry about the bullets bouncing around."

"YYEEEEAAAAHHH!!!" Two crazed women jumped on him from behind. They screamed and bit and clawed at his face. They beat on him with rocks and pulled him to the ground. I grabbed his rifle from him as he fell. The torch landed on the ground beside us. The shadows danced around as crazy as the women who were attacking him.

"OFF!" He threw them back.

I knelt on his chest and held the rifle above him. His gauze had been ripped off and the bright red slash across his jaw from the beating I had given him earlier opened up and bled down his cheek. He looked up at me in fear and for once, I don't think it was because of my appearance. I stopped myself for the briefest of moments. I threw the rifle aside. His eyes followed the gun. One swift strike was enough to render him unconscious. I was glad I didn't have to kill him.

The women ran to their babies. I could still hear fighting outside, but no gunshots. I led the women out of the cave, where we were immediately set upon by a group of men. They were on me at all sides. They threw the women and children aside and began just pounding me with stones and rifles. Their numbers scarcely allowed me to strike back, but it also lessened the severity of their own swings and prevented them from pulling a gun. I brought my knee up and popped someone in the crotch. I took advantage of the small opening to kick myself away from the group. I fell back and rolled into the cave opening.

"Get him!" I heard the sheriff shout.

They piled on me and grabbed my arms as I was on the floor. With one hand, I swung two of them over and into the wall as hard as I could manage. I got up to my knees. One man went out as his head cracked against the rocks. The other screamed and rolled up on the floor, his face bloodied from the impact. Two more men and Jimmy Plummer now beat on me. Jimmy was howling like a wolf with rabies. He had a broken pick handle in his hand that he stabbed and clubbed with, occasionally hitting the ground or another man. I forced myself up and grabbed the weapon from his hand. That left me open to two pile driving fists to my stomach and midsection. I bent over and fell backwards into the wall with the stick in my hands. The three men lunged at me. I busted the handle over the head of one of the men, and he fell aside. The other man dodged it by ducking down, allowing Jimmy an opening to elbow me in the teeth. I fell to my knees and heard a metallic click. The other man had locked one of the slave leggings to my wrist.

"RRAAAGH!" I roared like some sort of beast.

The two of them set upon me like they were cotton threshers, taking turns beating me about my face and body until I spit blood. I curled up and raised my leg around the man's neck and smashed his head down into the hard dirt floor. I'm not sure if his neck broke, but he stopped moving.

Jimmy was still screaming and crying and wailing like a man possessed. I continued to pull against the chain that was spiked into the stone wall. I pulled with more strength than any man, more strength than I should have been able to possess in this battered frame. It was Divine strength, not my strength, and I felt the spike move.

"I'm killin' the monster, Daddy," Jimmy screamed. "It's dyin'! It's dyin'!"

My hand flew out as the spike finally gave away. I flung the chain around Jimmy's neck with all the power that had just pulled a nail from solid rock. He choked and gagged and drooled all over me. He clawed at the chains as I hissed and pulled them tighter.

"Monster… fights… back!" I heard myself growl.

His eyes rolled back, and I threw him aside. He spun as the chain unraveled, and he landed in the shadows of the dying torchlight. I tried to catch my breath. I looked up through battered eyes to see the sheriff smiling down on me. His gun was mere inches from my face.

Click…

"It's ovah," he said.

BANG!

The shot rang out through the legs of the Spider Cave, but I never felt the bullet. I involuntarily closed my eyes at that final moment. I opened them only when I heard and felt the body falling next to me. It was Sheriff Plummer, face down, a bullet in the back of his head. A dark figure stood silent in the shadows at the entrance of the cave.

"Gl…glass man…?" I could hardly speak. "Griller?"

The man said nothing. He just stood there with his gun pointed, the last vestiges of smoke crawling up out of the barrel and into the still air. I crawled a few steps past the bodies of my attackers and pulled myself up at the fenceline. I walked like a drunken man and stood next to the man who had just saved my life. It was Deputy Jason Stone.

We stood there shoulder to shoulder, not looking at one another, not speaking. He looked straight ahead into the cave at the flickering torch. He showed no emotion. I looked out of the mouth of the cave into the shadows and stars beyond. We breathed in unison three times as he finally, eventually lowered his gun.

I staggered out into the cool night, where I was relieved to see no one standing. Most had fled into the safety of the night or were lying unconscious or worse around the entrance. I started to walk towards the treeline when a familiar voice called out.

"Yer dang lucky I'm outa' bullets, Alabaster Kid," Griller's voice echoed from the top of the hill.

"And *you* are lucky…" I tried to talk, but the strength had left me. I just threw down my hands and stumbled into the night, hunched down and depleted.

Somehow New Moon found me eventually. I don't know how long I walked in circles. With great effort, I climbed on his back. I slumped over onto his neck.

"You lead," I whispered.

CHAPTER TWENTY-THREE

When I awoke, there were fires. There were fires in my muscles and bones and skin. There was a campfire burning next to me, and there was a large ball of fire bearing down from the sky.

"Ak!" I shielded my eyes. "The sun!"

I was lying on a sand and pebble bank next to the river. I rolled off the blanket and kept rolling until I was shaded by some dead cattails.

"He's awake!" Lincoln stood up from his seat on a dead tree trunk that had washed ashore. He dropped his fishing rod in the sand.

Bandages covered my face, medical bandages. Someone had doctored me while I was out.

"Your sun cheaters." Severin stood over me with my specs in his hand. "We can take this to the trees. The sun hasn't been up all that long."

"I thought I was in Hell." I took the specs.

"Only sinners go to Hell." Severin helped me up.

"We are all sinners," I said. "Only those saved by grace…"

"Even half dead, he preaches." Golden Eagle put my arm around his neck and practically carried me into the shade.

As the three men led me into the shadows, I felt my strength returning. There was another fire in a clearing where they had pulled some blankets over some low branches. Several women and children mulled about, fixing up camp, frying fish and other things, doing various chores.

"Is everyone safe?" I asked.

116

"We don't know about everyone." Severin sat down next to the fire. He laid a couple of small blue gill in the ashes. "We may never know about everyone."

"My daughter is safe," Golden Eagle turned and raised his hand to his family, "and my aunt."

I sat on a log and looked at the food. The bandages itched like my wraps seldom did.

"Hungry?" Severin asked.

"As John in the Wilderness," I said. My mouth watered.

"I figured you would be."

A young girl ran up to me and put her arms around my neck.

"Thank you, Alabaster," she said in a near breathless voice. "Thank you!"

"That is enough, Mary." Golden Eagle sat next to me.

"Can he call me Walking Moon?" she asked her father. "After all, he walks in the moon." She looked into my eyes. "Your eyes are like the moon," she said. "That is my real name. Mary is my white name."

Golden Eagle looked over at us. He pulled his pipe from a bag on his belt. "No," he said.

His aunt scolded him in their language. He just grunted and lit his pipe.

"Saqqara." The woman placed her hand on her chest and looked at me.

"A british man from Egypt was very kind to her," Golden Eagle said. "He was from Saqqara, Egypt, so she chose that as her white name."

"Doesn't sound like any white name I've ever heard." Severin scooped his dented coffee cup into a large boiling pot of vegetables on the fire.

"Doesn't matter." Golden Eagle puffed furiously. "She doesn't speak the white man's language anyway."

I peeled off a large bandage. My skin was smooth beneath it, but covered in salve and a large bump.

"There were stores of food at the cave," Golden Eagle continued. "I went back and got some. Everyone was gone. All the bodies had been removed, even the Ferrell boy."

"I am Lincoln." The large man walked into camp with a string of fish. Two women came over and took them from him. "I can never thank you enough."

I stood and shook his battered hands. My own were still sore. He sat down opposite the fire, next to the shovel he had used in the escape the previous night.

"What will happen now?" I kicked some mud from my feet into the fire.

"We have your guns." Golden Eagle pointed his fingers like a gun at Saqqara. She nodded and walked off. "I'm afraid your knife saw much action and did not survive."

"The Agency will come in and clean up, I imagine. Or the army." Severin handed me a cup of hot stew. "Maybe run down those who have fled and deal with those who haven't."

"No, I… Mmmm…" I downed the entire cup of food and leaned in to scoop some more.

Others came in with old cups and plates and anything that would hold the food, including pieces of driftwood. There were several families. All of them laid hands on me and thanked me. Saqqara brought me my guns. They had been cleaned.

"Wait!" I said, and everyone froze. "You thanked me, but we mustn't forget the One who saved us all!"

"Amen," Lincoln said. "Let us pray."

We all stood and bowed our head. Lincoln led a prayer of earnest thanks, a prayer that must have been like that of Moses. Many cried, myself included. When he finished, I looked up to a family of faces. Only Golden Eagle had left the group.

"Veil was founded by our fathers." Lincoln sat back down. "After the war, a group of freed slaves came to Veil and carved it out of pristine prairie. They named it after an old hymn."

"The one you were singing." I looked off to see Golden Eagle walking to the river. I took another large swallow of food.

"Yes," Lincoln looked into the flames, "but then white folks came and started filling up the town and taking over. Pretty soon we couldn't even attend our own school. We tried to fight back. We placed a warning on the sign."

"From Lamentations," I said. "I saw it."

"But they didn't heed it," he said. "Before long, the old ways took back over. We feared for the safety of our families. Some of the older folks, God help us, even looked fondly at the old times."

"We'll put a stop to this," Severin said.

"Never again." Lincoln shook his head and picked up his shovel. "It won't happen again."

After a time, I wandered off over by the river to a tree that Golden Eagle was tapping his pipe against. He leaned back and took a draw. Severin walked with me.

"I wonder what will happen now with these people," I said.

"Nothing." Severin kicked some dead grass at the base of the tree. "They're free. They can do what they want."

"How are they going to find a life after they've been in chains?" I said. "It's not like they all have farms waiting for them in the next county."

"It's not our responsibility," Severin looked out over the stream in the distance. He stepped over and picked up the chain that they had removed from my wrist, "We helped them get out of chains, but it's not the agency's place or the government's place to tell them what to do next."

"They can live off the land," Golden Eagle said. "That is what my family did after we were broken apart by your government, the one whose place it is not to tell us what to do."

I took the chain from Severin and held it in my hand. It seemed so heavy the night before. I pulled my arm back and heaved the shackle as far as I could. It splashed into the rapids of the river and disappeared in the whitecaps.

"You can form a new tribe with all these people," Severin smiled and joked.

"Perhaps I might." Golden Eagle walked past Severin and blew smoke into his face. "Hold this." He handed Severin his pipe. He reached around his own neck and pulled the claw necklace out from where it was tucked in his shirt.

"Griller is still out there," I said. "I'm going after him."

"Do you need my help?" Severin puffed on Golden Eagle's pipe.

"Do you need *our* help?" Golden Eagle snatched his pipe back. "You have an army of helpers here. You are a part of this tribe."

"You can take care of our tribe." I put my hand on Golden Eagle's shoulder and then looked at Severin. "And you can help the cavalry clean up this mess."

Severin nodded.

Golden Eagle took off the claw from around his neck and handed it to me. "Take this," he said. "It will bring you much luck. My grandfather had it when we escaped the army."

"I can't..."

"Bad form." Golden Eagle placed the claw in my hand. "It will help you move silently and swiftly. You can bring it back once you have Griller."

"Didn't do much good for the eagle," Severin said.

"Ill rest up for a few days before I get out on the trail after Griller." I placed the claw around my neck. "I'll be out there once the full moon rises."

END

THE REAL LIFE ALABASTER KID

The real Peter Tentman, aka the Alabaster Kid, was born around 1881 in northwest Missouri. His parents were Richard and June Tentman. His father was a butcher and a rancher. Peter did have albinism, but it was nothing like the strangeness of the fiction. He was sensitive to the sun, but had no monstrous deformities or heightened senses. That's all just the myth built up out of superstition and fear. He himself helped build on that myth when he first was a member of a state militia and later worked with the Bureau of Prohibition to hunt down and destroy illegal stills and rum runners. In between that time, there were about four years in the early 1900's when he was a self employed or contracted bounty hunter. He would sometimes work for bondsmen. Other times he would search on his own, based on wanted posters. It didn't pay well and often led to dead ends or weeks of boredom punctuated by sudden intense life-threatening drama. It was difficult to track down someone from just the information on a poster. The bail bondsmen usually had more reliable information and insights. Plus it was difficult for Peter to blend in for his detective work with him being not only albino, but also over six feet tall.

Unfortunately, it is believed that he never really wore cloth strips like a mummy even though every drawn depiction of him shows him wearing the strips, and this was especially prevalent after the discovery of King Tut's tomb in 1922. He denied wearing the strips in several interviews when he was older. He did often wear a large hat to shade his face and occasionally he wore a bandana over the lower part of his face. He also often wore sunglasses but not red ones.

He was a deeply religious man and only agreed to marry Mary Smith after she and her entire family was baptized. They were Native Americans that claimed Christianity in their own way, replete with traditional Indian customs and symbols. Peter Tentman would have none of that. Mary's original name was Walking Moon, but her father made her change it when she was young so that she could better integrate into the white man's world.

Peter was a voracious reader who took full advantage of the library. He also donated many books and had a large library of his own. At the height of the depression, he organized the remodeling of a grain storage building along the Missouri River in St. Joseph. It was converted into a library, using most of the books that made up his personal collection. Just a few years later, the entire structure and all its contents were lost in a flood. "It was like losing a child," Peter said in his unpublished memoirs. He wrote at least twelve books, mostly Biblical studies. At least six were published. One was a small book called *The Evils of Drink*. It was meant to be carried with missionaries and evangelists to be given to drunkards to remind them of the horrors their habit would wreak and to remind them to turn back temptation and spit in Satan's eye. It had several colorful illustrations and is highly collectible today.

He settled down to a small farm in Andrew County, Missouri. There he had a daughter and a son. He kept several animals. He had an affinity towards them. Aside from multiple cats and dogs and birds, he was known to have milking cows, horses, goats, pigs, and sheep. He had not a lot of them, but a few of each, all named, all with free reign of the farm regardless of the damage done to the crops. Mary did insist on fencing off the garden though, and the chickens were kept in a large coop. One of Peter's unpublished books was filled with stories about the antics of his animals.

Peter lived to be nearly 84. He passed away in February 1965, having witnessed a new world come into being in his lifetime. Mary saw an even greater change as she was eight years younger than Peter and lived to be 96. She was working in her garden well into her nineties. She passed gently at her son's house on June 7th, 1985.

In his lifetime, he took small commissions from the dozens of thrillers and westerns written about the Alabaster Kid. There were even detective novels and science fiction/fantasy novels in the later years. He didn't write them or claim to even read them but given his proclivity for the written word, I would be surprised if he didn't scan one or two. His character was famously a guest star in one of the Slipknot crime noir novels and was even a star of a short lived CBS radio program, *The Adventures of the Alabaster Kid, Bounty Hunter!*, which mixed western adventure with suspense and horror.

When television came calling for interviews, Peter always wore his handkerchief and dark glasses to keep the mystery up. Still, the public always envisioned him in the mummy wraps. That visualization was mostly thanks to artist Alvin Chesterfield, who was responsible for most of the incredible painted covers in the early MedVed Press westerns that were reprinted for a new generation in the sixties by Monarch Press. Also, when Alan Fedderman portrayed the Alabaster Kid in the Pinnacle Studios silent short, he sported the wrap look. Only snippets of those films have survived, but they are action filled and incredible. Apparently, there was one where Fedderman had eyebrows painted on over the wrappings, but none of those are around today.

This novel was written with the knowledge and permission of Peter Tentman's direct grandchildren, Frederick Tentman and Mindy Tentman Brown. I thank them for their insights, their hospitality, and their cooperation.

Finally, it is not really documented where the name *the Alabaster Kid* came from originally. Peter Tentman alternately revealed and denied that he had anything to do with it. Ian Braun has the first known fiction of the Alabaster Kid (*The Alabaster Kid and the Curse of the Lizard King*, Independent Parcels, Pub. 1901), but he said he was inspired by a newspaper article about Tentman and some other men regarding the Spanish American War. The article has never been found however, and Peter Tentman didn't serve in the Spanish American War, at least where history or Peter Tentman revealed. Braun said the article specifically mentioned the ragged young militiaman, the Alabaster Kid, who saved the American flag and brought the bullet-scarred symbol through the fray. Something tells me that would make a good novel. Regardless of his origin, the Alabaster Kid will stand as one of the world's most enduring characters as long as people yearn for stories of action and adventure.

Many of his adventures were fictionalized in cheap novelizations at the turn of the century. Among the early ones include:

The Alabaster Kid and the Curse of the Lizard King (Independent Parcels)
The Night of the Lost Moon (Chittington)
Gold and Red on Champion Bluff (Chittington)
The Kansas City Gamble (Chittington)
The Alabaster Kid and the Oil Baron Murders (MedVed Press)
The Alabaster Kid and the Flying Steam Engine (MedVed Press)
The Alabaster Kid and the Sunday Morning Gang (MedVed Press)
The Circus Rustlers (Brawn/Campbell)
The Lull Before the Dawn (Brawn/Campbell)
Midnight Spirits (Brawn Ass.)
The Falling Piano of Culver Street (Pepperpot)

Silent film star Alan Fedderman played the Alabaster Kid in at least six short films from Pinnacle Studios. None of these films survive in their entirety.

ABOUT THE AUTHOR

I grew up in Missouri. It's where I live now, right between Kansas City and St. Joseph near the border of Kansas. I have the Alabaster Kid operate out of St. Joseph because of its importance to the early west, but by the time of this story, St. Joe was on a slow slide down from its former prominence. I was raised on a farm, tilling dirt, chopping and splitting wood to burn in the winter. I was born in 1965, long enough ago to still see some of the evidence of a generation past as it disintegrated into the modern age. A great deal of my writing comes from there.

Oftentimes at book signings, I would get requests for westerns. There seems to be a natural yearning for the rural stories from the people still living it, or only a generation or two removed. I consider myself amongst them, proudly so. In any case, I thought it might be a nice change of pace to write a western, but my specialties were more in characters than setting. A true western makes the place a character all its own. I wasn't sure I was up to the task. Then I met Ron Fortier, a leader of a literary movement that was beginning to be called neo-pulp. I have been fortunate enough to have some stories accepted by his Airship 27 Enterprises. When I recognized the vast amounts of pulp westerns that were written for decades, I knew what I had to do.

Out of that mixture of western and pulp came this neo-pulp collection. Some writers begin with the story. Some start with the genre or the place. I started with the characters and let the world move all around them. That's not always how I write a book, but it was how I wrote this one. The Alabaster Kid has many secrets, and only a few are revealed here. I plan on many more stories with our pasty bounty hunter.

Now, Slipknot is pure pulp. Maybe there's a little noir mixed in, but it's a lot of action. Obviously, fans of the Spirit and Midnight can see the resemblance, but I wanted to take it in a different direction. It is a satire of the masked detective genre. This is a tortured man led by his demons, who nevertheless tries to be on the side of the angels. As a matter of fact, he would rather be with the angels than here on earth.

Striving for Heaven while pulling chains and carrying stones in the dirt is a commonality between these two characters, Alabaster Kid and Slipknot. Whether they succeed in rising above their own darkness, and what would happen to them if they did, will take more than these stories can give.

I've recently helped found a new comic book company, InDEL-Lible Comics, with a couple of other gentlemen, James Ludwig, our EIC, and Daerick Gross Sr., art director and illustrator of both of the fine covers on this book. Check us out online, and look for our books coming soon on Amazon. *All-New Popular Comics* is our first title. The Alabaster Kid may make an appearance in an upcoming issue.

I have several other books available. There is a list in the book. If you enjoy this book, you will surely enjoy them as well. Drop me a line on Facebook and let me know what you think. Like my pages—Tradeofthetricks and typomagazine1.

Keep an eye out for my next book, a collection of short stories about a sweet little American town in 1950 and the "interesting" characters that live there. I'm joined by some wonderful authors. It's called *Welcome to Honeycomb, USA!*

Check out these other books by
David Noe

Trade of the Tricks: The Tricks' Brand

Living In Someone Else's House

Odds and Ends (But Mostly Odds)

The Notions of Minsa Van Whey/Psychic Biker

Guide To Ghosts: Seeing the Truth Through the Spiritual Veil

Scanner Code

Kin

Voices in My Pen

New Things Among the Old

With a Twist

The Thrill of Drowning

See all titles by David Noe on Amazon:

http://www.amazon.com/David-Noe/e/B00YNQZVAQ

ABOUT THE INTERIOR ARTIST

Paul Tuma is an illustrator with a background in 1930s pulp comics, who worked previously on Dan Turner, Hollywood Detective, The Twilight Zone, and Tales of the Green Hornet. He has also worked in humor cartooning, doing satire for CNSNews.com, CATO Institute, and CRACKED magazine. In recent years he has concentrated on indie horror fantasy material and book illustration projects, such as KING KONG for Starwarp Concepts. He is currently developing adult coloring books, westerns, and jungle comics for anthology publications.

ABOUT THE COVER ARTIST

  With over 50 years in the commercial art and illustration field, and holding several awards, Dærick Gröss Sr. has worked as an illustrator, cartoonist, instructor, and art director.

  As an illustrator, Dærick started his career after Commercial Art School in Cincinnati, and worked for a couple of advertising agencies. He soon moved on to a television station art-department (Scripps-Howard/WCPO), creating sets, camera cards, and promo material. From there he moved on to a daily newspaper, The Cincinnati Post, where he was the principal illustrator/cartoonist (and later, art director) creating illustrations and caricatures that are now becoming very collectible, particularly his full page caricatures of 'The Big Red Machine' World Series. After three plus years, he shifted his location to Los Angeles, where, coming off of a one-man show in a New York gallery, he started his free-lance career with The LA Times, continuing his newspaper illustrations, and Gold's Gym as his initial clients. Over the next ten years, he had projects with all the major movie studios as well as clients in the music, magazine and corporate worlds. Among the works done are the very collectable posters for "Not of This Earth", "Chillers", "Hollywood's New Blood", and the "1980 Mr. America" competition. It was during this time that, he founded (and still maintains) 'Studio G' as his own illustrative art and production house, along with his new 'The G-Spot' studio for his cartoons and humor.

It was as he turned 40 that he entered the world of comic books, and soon after, RPG. In these industries, he has painted, drawn, and inked for Marvel, DC, Image, Malibu, Studio G, Heroic, Revolutionary, Chaos, Innovation, and Topps, Fantasy Flight, Game of Thrones and numerous other companies. His best-selling work includes the series Anne Rice's "The Vampire Lestat" for Innovation (followed by "Forbidden Planet"); "Necroscope" for MalibuComics; "Batman: Two-Face" for DC Comics, and "Bloodwulf" for Image Comics. He was also the principle artist for most of Marvel's CYBER COMICS, their entrance into the digital world. Dærick also did all the art for the best-selling sex instruction book, "Guide To Getting It On" (now in its 8th Edition).

Currently, Dærick is still doing a 'little bit of everything', including art directing and slave labor for InDELLible Comics.

Among several illustration and art achievement awards is the West Coast Comic Club's prestigious Russ Manning Award, now managed by Comicon International.

Check out these books from
Amazing Things Press

Amazing Things Press

DAVID NOE

SLIPKNOT

Book design by Julie L. Casey
Cover art by Dærick Gröss Sr.
Interior art by Paul Tuma

*This book is a work of fiction. Any names, characters, or incidents
are the product of the author's imagination and are used fictitiously.
Any resemblance to actual events, locales, or persons, living or dead is
purely coincidental.*

ISBN 978-1945667435

Printed in the United States of America.

For more information, visit

www.authordavidnoe.weebly.com
or
www.amazingthingspress.com

We tell ourselves we can do it. We tell ourselves we are strong. We have no other choice. We fight the battles in our path with every tool at our disposal. We have to keep going, to keep moving, to keep dealing with the strife.

It's better than the alternative.

There are people who would cut us down. There are evil selfish men who would take everything we have, just to see us lose it. We have to be steadfast. We have to keep trying. Surely God would never allow more than we could handle. Surely there has to be an end to the night, a new dawn, a new chance… one more smile…

Runyan Mann was at the end of his rope. His family was taken. His home destroyed. The evil overtook him, yet still he fought. They broke him physically. They crushed his soul, but still he fought. They ground him down until there was no more up, and there he was…

at the end of his rope… literally…

What happens when a man steps down, when gravity takes it course and the only thing stopping him from the stained wooden floor is a length of hemp tied to a ceiling beam? What happens when a man gives in to the final call and welcomes the embrace? What becomes of that man when even that fate is denied, when the beam breaks before the neck? When he rises, half crazed and half dead after his mind has already checked out, what stands in his place?

What becomes of Mann when the surrender fails? How do we continue when we are denied even our final rest?

We let the Slipknot take his place.

Chapter One
Beans of Escape

You are in so much luck...

I am currently being handed my face one fistful at a time by a rat-like little punk called the Beak. I reckon he got that cute little nickname onnacounta' his hooknose that sticks out way past those tiny black dots he calls eyes. See, he's got me tied to a chair and he's trying to extract a little info from me. His boss, some loser that hasn't yet learned the proper way to lose, is the king of this town. His name is Indigo Marino, and he seems to think I know the whereabouts of a little trinket he's got the hots for. It's part of his mystical collection of hoo-doo junk he's been paying big bucks for. It's called the Golden Claw, and it's supposed to grant you good luck and the ability to hide like a ninja and probably a hundred other fake magic powers. Trouble is, almost nobody knows where it is or what it looks like. Guess it works pretty good.

This pipsqueak's been wailing on me on and off for two days now. I've been through this kind of thing before, you know. He's just working up to the harder stuff, taking his time. They always have to work up to the harder stuff because despite popular belief, I'm pretty good at keeping my mouth

shut. He's just lucky the Slipknot's not here. Then he'd be talking outa' the other side of his beak.

And me? Yeah, I'm Runyan Mann, PI. I've been taking this sort of crap for over three years now, hunting down cheating hubbies, scoping for lost pearls, chasing down Marino's thugs. He kinda' has it in for me. I've been skulking around Veil City in a domino mask calling myself the Slipknot. It's starting to have an effect. Oh, don't get me wrong, crime's just as bad as it ever was, but I'm getting attacked by a lot more thugs than ever before.

Last year, Slipknot and Marino finally had it out up in Marino's penthouse in the Zephyr Building. Slipknot took a couple bullets. Marino took a dive through a plate glass window and four stories of glass ceilings. I haven't seen much of either one of them since, but I've sure been feeling their presence.

Now Marino's men shoot at me from the shadows, and the Slipknot tightens around my mind. Nineteen thirty-nine has been a bad year for us all. None of us can hit our mark. I've been one step behind Marino's mob for the last half-dozen artifacts he's tried to snatch. Sure, most of his prizes are dead ends, but his trail is usually cold by the time I get a whiff of it.

Let me tell you why you're lucky. You see, when I start taking the strap, I have to find a way to deal with the pain. I like to narrate, like on the radio but in my head... usually. I mean, I know you're not real, but you don't know you're not real, so you might as well sit back and enjoy my pain. It's more than I can do right now. I can try to block it out, take a nap in this chair I'm tied up in, but my Fedora is over on the

2

little wooden table up next to the stove along with my Browning… oh, and the Slipknot's little black mask.

"Come on, Mann! You might as well eat some a' this swill." Beak is shoving old beans in my face. I'd sooner eat rat droppings off the floor, which is what the spoon looks like it was last used for. Plus, those beans smell like feet… boiling feet.

I can feel a loose tooth and a trickle of blood coming outa' the corner of my mouth, out around my 'laugh' lines, oozing out and sticking in my stubble. My hair's down over my eye, so I can't exactly tell if it's blurry because of the long black strands I usually keep slicked up under my hat or because of the stylish brass knuckles he was massaging me with earlier.

"It ain't like yer gonna be able ta' chew once I finish knockin' alla' yer teeth down yer throat."

The Beak is known for his sense of humor. By the way, that's what passes for a sense of humor in his circles. Unfortunately, it's one of those serious jokes, the kind where the punchline is an actual punch. I humor him and take a bite, but I sneer when I do it so that he don't think I'm any too happy about it.

The real ploy here though, is what's happening under my formerly nice dark blue jacket. I've been sweating for hours, pulling on these ropes, but I'm no fool. Ropes have never been my friend. You may think that's ironic given my attire, but I don't know the meaning of the word. You might see this noose I wear around my neck instead of a necktie, and you might think I like ropes. You'd be wrong. You see, it's advertisement. I'm like a hangman. You don't escape the hangman.

3

Well… most people don't.

"Atta' boy! Take a big ol' bite! Yer gonna be here a while unless you tell me where you hid the Golden Claw."

Oh, didn't I tell you? Marino thinks I got the Golden Claw. I don't know where he gets his information. I say, I usually don't know where he gets his information. In this case, he got it from me—not me straight, of course. He got it from a guy who got it from another guy who got it from Melanie Singer most probably. She's the dame I slip alla' my secrets to, including the ones I want to get out to alla' the wrong people. She's good at getting to alla' the wrong people, mostly because she is one. I let slip in a tender moment about this solid gold cast claw, and how it was brought up from Mexico by that railroad tycoon, Rutherford Miner. It was part of them Aztec rituals where they used to rip out human hearts. She takes real well to the bit about ripping out hearts. Well, old Rutherford fell on hard times, I heard, or rather, hard times fell on him, and he sadly misplaced the claw. I'm keeping it for a friend who 'inherited' it.

Marino's gang rifled through my office more than once before deciding to go to the source. That's when the Beak here got his current houseguest, if you can call this one room fire hazard apartment a house.

"KKKK-kk-kk-k…" The old wooden chair doesn't much like the ropes either, or the way I'm pulling against them.

The Beak is busy cackling and throwing burning spoons of beans at me and stuffing my mouth full to overflowing like I'm some Thanksgiving turkey he was trying to interrogate. "Ha-HAA! Whaddyoo think a' my cooking, eh, Mann?"

4

I mean, I have to now, don't I? With an opening line like that, I just have to. He sticks his ugly puss down in my face, and I let it rip. I spit the whole sloppy mess all over him. He jumps back and cusses up a storm. Then he backhands me a good one. All the while, I'm working those ropes. He grabs a dishcloth, and I lean into the chair, throwing my weight back and stretching out as hard as I can.

"Nee-AAAH!" I bust my arms and legs loose as the chair pops apart. I kick Beak in the stomach as I go down, almost like I'd planned it.

"I've had BETTER!" I shout as I crash down on a pile of broken chair limbs.

My hands are numb now from the ropes, way past the prickly pin stage, but I can still make a fist. My gloves help some by giving me something between my skin and the ropes. There are times when I wish my neck woulda' had that protection back in my dark days. Then there are days like this when I sometimes think it might be better all around if the noose woulda' done it's job.

The Beak and I both look over to the filthy gas stove. It's not the pot of beans we're looking at. It's my Browning perched on the edge of the table about to jump. I just knocked it a little closer to the edge when I broke the chair. It's right next to the flame now, almost touching it. Somebody ought to do it the courtesy of moving it away from the heat. There's nothing worse than firing a gun when you don't mean to.

"Yer done for, pal." Beak blows some baked beans outa' his nose and dives for the piece.

I'm still on the floor with broken bits of chair tied to me and my hands behind my back. I swing my foot around in an arc, using the rope like a cat o' nine tails, complete with a chunk of splintered chair leg at the end.

"AAK!" It smacks Beak in the side of the head and sends him stumbling towards the front door. He lays there in the dark filth of the old apartment, bleeding on a wooden floor that's seen a lot worse. The single bulb swings from the ceiling, making the whole room swirl with shadows.

I hop up and scan the room for a handy knife. I've gotta get free of these ropes and get use of my hands. I can't even get my gun or my hat or my...

"Fire," I practically sigh the word.

I turn around and back up to the stove. There's only so long my leather gloves can help me. It's way too soon that they catch on fire and allow the blue flame of the stovetop to start cooking away the layers of my skin.

"NNnnnggg...!" I grit my teeth hard enough to bite the ropes in two. Too bad they're around my wrists and not between my teeth.

"GyyAAHH!" I'm free! I'm on fire, but I'm free.

I start swinging like a big league pitcher setting up a knuckle ball. The edge of my sleeve catches flame. I slam both hands down deep into the pot of boiling beans. My God, that hurts.

To say that I scream loud enough to wake the dead would be one of those gross exaggerations, but it might be true enough to say that I screamed loud enough to wake the unconscious. While I've got my charbroiled hands up in front of my

6

sweaty shaking bloody face, gaping at them like a dog begging for bacon, the Beak has woken up from his little nap and has found a length of wire under what used to be the chair. See, I'm so caught up in my peeling fingers that I don't even see him get up. I'm so busy being on fire that I don't hear him pull a wire from the pile. I don't notice him rise up above me. In fact, it's not until the wire is around my neck that I'm able to get over the pain of boiled beans and knuckles.

"The CLAW!" Beak squawks. "Where is the Golden Claw?"

"Akk-kk-kk..." I answer back. It's the best I can manage at such short notice.

Beak gets right up in my ear. I'm trying desperately to get my charred hands under that wire. Guess I'm gonna have another scar to go with all the others around my twisted neck.

"Marino says to do whatever it takes to find that claw, Mann." He pulls even tighter, jerking back and practically picking me up offa' the floor. "Whatever it takes!"

I pull myself forward despite his weight, despite the pain and the choking and the light-headedness.

"I... k-k-k... TOLD you..." I'm literally slobbering all over the stove and the pot of beans.

I fall back with a sudden jerk and ram my elbow into the Beak's gut.

"HORFF!" His grip slips off the wire.

"I..." I wrap my cracked fingers around the cracked handle of the pot of beans. I swear my fingers crackle, "DON'T..."

7

In that instant, the Beak just kinda' stands there stupid. It's just a split second. It's not like he has time to do anything else. It's just that he's really good at standing there stupid. We both know what's about to happen. Neither one of us can stop it.

"...KNOW!" I scream and slam the entire mess into his face.

Beans splatter the wall and the floor and the ceiling and the Beak.

SPANNNG! is the sound of a pot full of beans breaking a large nose.

I stand over the Beak with the pot still in my hands. He's crawling backwards, wiping at the blood flowing from his face and mixing with the bean juice. He's whimpering a little.

"I'm searching for it myself." I drop the pot and lean down into the Beak's face. I grab him by the front of his shirt. Ironically, it's a wife beater. Guess I do know the meaning of the word.

"You tell Marino to lay off, see?" I look him dead on in those beady little eyes.

"You dode udderstad, Madd," the Beak squeaks. "Id's eider youse 'er me."

I frown and spit a bean out to the side.

"Ad it ai't godda be me!" Beak spreads a large bloody grin and grabs hold of the noose around my neck.

"kktt..." that really shouldn't have taken me by surprise.

He pulls it tight with renewed energy, like he's got me now, like this is what he's been after all along. Remember how I said he was good at the stupid look? I pull back and stand up. The Beak comes with me, but he falls back against

the door when my breakaway noose breaks away and rips my shirt open down to my belly button. Now my scars are out in the open. Ropes can cut like knives sometimes, and the scars last a lifetime.

I reach out with one hand and grab him by the shirt again. "You think I'd be so dumb as to let myself be choked with my own noose?" I pull my other fist back. "I've done this before, you know."

"Nod agedd!" Beak shields his face and turns his head. "Madd, please! Please dode hurd me, PLEASE!"

I pick him up, and man, I'm ready to let him have it, but he's got a point.

"You're right," I drop him. He crumples to the floor. "I can't do this."

I turn my back on the little vermin, forgetting just how quick the devious little gangster can turn, forgetting that my gun is now laying at my feet, almost in reach of the Beak.

"I can't live my life like this." I go over to the only things left on the table. I put on my hat and pick up the little domino mask. It's smooth, almost slippery, like it's felt or something. "But I know someone who can," I slip the mask over my eyes and see things all different.

Where the mask was slippery in my torn fingers, it sticks like glue to Slipknot's face. "This ends now," Slipknot says and turns around to my own gun being pointed at him.

"Lass chazz, Madd!" the Beak spits out. "I aid playid doe moe! Gib up da Golded Claw 'er die ride heah."

"Do you feel it, Beak?" Slipknot turns back to the fire and talks in a voice way calmer than it has a right to be.

"Wh-whaddo you…?"

The Slipknot steps closer to the Beak. The Beak backs up in surprise. I mean, *he* has the gun. He's the one in control.

"You feel the tightening in your gut…" Slipknot puts his fist over his stomach, "the catch in your throat?"

The Beak holds the gun out at arm's length, almost touching Slipknot, and Slipknot strolls right up to it.

"Like it's over?" He sneers at the Beak. "Like the noose is around your neck?"

"I godda doe, Madd," The Beak is shaking his head and crying and rocking back and forth from foot to foot. "I *gooda* fide out!"

"There is no Mann here." The Slipknot just reaches out and around the gun.

BANG! the Beak shoots into the floor as Slipknot rips it away from him.

"AAH!" The Beak jumps back in fear.

"There's only the SLIPKNOT!" He grabs the Beak by the neck and throws him up against the wall. Old cigarette-stained pictures crash to the floor.

"Tell Marino," Slipknot's jaw is tight as he slaps the Beak across his already broken face, "that his days of terror are over. I'm back in action!"

He throws the Beak on the floor and starts beating the stuffing out of him.

"And NONE of his talismans…!"

Beak is screaming and begging, but Slipknot just keeps on pounding and breaking and smashing.

"…can protect him from ME!"

Eventually, he stops flailing, long after the Beak is able to protest.

"Never mind," Slipknot regains his composure and picks up the broken noose and useless gun off the floor. "I think he'll get the message."

He picks up my jacket off the cot and slings it across his shoulder, and he leaves the door open as he walks off into the night.

Chapter Two
Drinking Out of My Hands

It turns out that Slipknot likes to drink, which is a real shame because so do I, and your body can take only so much alcohol before it becomes a bloody Mary. I wake up sometime in some afternoon. It may be the next day. It may be the next week. It depends on how much work the Slipknot has on his list.

My noose tie is lying on a chair in the office, all alone. I decide to leave it there and button up my wrinkled shirt. I'm sitting at my desk, wondering why I even have a bed. It's just a fold out couch in my office anyway. I can't live in my apartment. Too many bad memories live there. There's a few G's on the desk in front of me. He must have collected some overdue bills. That's good, onnacounta' I got a few of my own I gotta take care of, mostly at Ice Pix. I decide to head on down there, pay off my tab, and start a new one. There's nothing like a nice fresh tab to make a man decide to drink. Bippy'll be glad to see me, well, glad to serve me. There ain't nobody glad to see me.

The place used to be called Llatches Bar and Grill, and I think it still is for tax purposes. Alla' us regulars call it Ice Pix after the last bar tender that was there before Bippy. He was

well loved by everyone, even when he'd bounce the drunks and loudmouths by threatening them with an ice pick. He even had to use it a time or two. Bippy keeps a spare ice pick, but it just ain't the same. There's a tragic story involving Ice Pix, me, Marino, Slipknot, and a pile of dead hookers, but I don't feel like narrating it right now. My head's pounding and my mouth is dry. I need something to lubricate them both and to staunch the taste of old beans and fresh blood. Suffice to say, we still call it Ice Pix, and the cardboard sign on the door still backs us up.

"What day is this?" I mumble as I walk through the door.

"Tuesday." Bippy wipes the empty bar. "Afternoon."

"Thank God," I say to his scowling scarred face. "I didn't miss the meeting with my client."

"What'd I say about meeting clients here in the bar?" Bippy sticks a toothpick in his mouth.

"This should get me caught up on my tab." I plop a wad of bills on the bar.

"Your regular meeting spot is waiting for you in the back, Mr. Mann." Bippy smiles and starts counting the dough. "Pleasure doing business with you, and have a nice day."

"Speaking of doing business with you," I meander off, "let's start up another tab, will ya'? Bring me something strong and stupid."

"It's your liver, bud." Bippy looks up at the clock.

"Like I'm worried about my liver." I look down at my bandaged hands. "I'll die of lead poisoning long before that."

"You been pounding the pavement?" Bippy jokes at my mauled mitts.

13

"Just bring the drink and leave the jokes to your mirror." I walk off to a nice smelly dark corner booth.

It starts raining in the city, and I'm glad I'm in a place I can get wet. There's nothing worse than being dry in the rain. Speaking of wet, I hear some movement slipping around in the back room. Since it's just me and Bippy in the bar, I'm pretty sure I know who's back there. She's in pretty early for someone who stays out so late.

"Melanie in the back?" I look up when Bippy brings the drink.

"Sounds like an intimate situation." He sets the glass down on the well-stained table. "What two consenting adults do ain't none a' my beeswax."

"Innuendo at this time of the day?"

"Innuendo… Inna back… I don't care where." He laughs and walks off, swatting his bar towel at flies.

I peel the bandages back offa' my hands, and my God, the pain. Guess I shoulda' figured it's a tad hurtful to scrape that many layers of skin off your hands this soon. I grab the cold glass of scotch with both slabs and let the ice melt between my fingers. Usually, I don't give it time to get watered down, but this is a special occasion. I shake with involuntary spasms as the cool glass both soothes and aches. I down the drink and feel the burns it absorbed from my hands building a fire in my stomach.

"Bippy!"

"Yeah, yeah."

"Little early, even for you, ain't it?" Her voice carries through the curtains, sounding like a cross between Mae West and a purring cat.

"Takes the edge off," I hiss. "I may need these paws later."

"Not as fists, surely." Melanie glides over and places her delicate fingers on my shoulder. "I'm sure we could find better uses for them."

"You're already in an evening gown." I look over out of the corner of my eyes. Then I down the last of my drink. "Little early for both of us, I'd say. Bippy, that drink!"

"I got it, softball." She makes this move that just touches the glass and it's outa' my hands. It's a move she's perfected.

"Don't call me softball." I lightly blow on my hands and close my eyes.

"Make it two." She holds the rim of her glass with her thumb and two fingers, sticking her pinky out. She slides it over to Bippy on the polished bar where he's already standing with two drinks on a silver platter.

"I'll bring it right over," he says.

She slinks back over on high heels. There's something in her smile that's awfully sad for a smile.

"I'm just trying on my gown for tonight's performance." She slips right next to me in the booth. "Whaddya think, Runyan?"

"I think you still don't have enough rouge to cover up that shiner." I stare at the table.

15

Melanie looks up and away in embarrassment. Bippy stands there at our table in silence, looking down on both of us. He sets the drinks down and walks away.

"Oleander back in town or are Marino's boys treating you rough again?" I take a swig. "I need to have a word with them?"

"Better'n not being treated at all, Runyan." Melanie looks down into her glass.

"I wouldn't be so sure," I say. "They got some poor mark they want you to stab inna' back?"

"I don't want to talk about it." She sets her drink down. "You wouldn't understand. You really wouldn't."

"Fine."

"…"

"I suppose I gotta shave and change before my meeting." I swish the last lonely drink around the bottom of the glass.

"Change?" Melanie sits up straight all startled and spills a splash of scotch on the table. It soaks it right up. "You mean, like… What do you mean?"

"My clothes?" I yank on my torn filthy bloody shirt. "In case you hadn't noticed the smell…"

"I noticed it!" Bippy dries my old glass with a rag.

"Nobody asked you!" I push my dead glass back. "And what did I say about listening in on my meetings?"

"Same thing I said about even having meetings." He places the glass with the others, "Don't."

"Did you, um…" Melanie places her hand on my thigh with a delicacy that betrays the heaviness of the question. "Did Marino get his prize?"

I turn my head and look her straight in the eyes. She looks back for only a moment before she has to look away. She pulls her hand back too, and I keep looking clean into her. She stands up and sets her drink down, then rubs her hands together like she's got lotion on them.

"I need to change too." She walks off quickly. Her heels clack all the way into the back room.

"Yeah, you do," my voice says out loud, but real quiet.

I down her drink and stand up. I straighten my jacket and fidget with my torn shirt. I head for the door and the day beyond.

"Hey," Bippy puts his hands down on the bar, "what about…"

"Put it on my tab," I say. "I'm expecting company at seven."

"And what time will you be here?"

"About seven-thirty." I walk out the door. "Wouldn't want to spoil their expectations."

Chapter Three
Meeting of the Mines

The long black hearse arrives just before seven. His dark Indian girl gets out first. I don't figure she's even old enough to be in a bar. She opens the door to the back of the car, while the driver, a big hulking black man in a suit that was made for a smaller hulking man, lifts Tentman out through the side back door.

Mr. Tentman is impeccably dressed in a black three-piece suit and a wide brim. He's taken to this wooden wheel chair that the girl gets out of the back. She covers his lap with a blanket and all the while, he doesn't move a muscle. Under that suit and all over his body, he's wrapped like King Tut or Boris Karloff. I'm across the street at the newsstand, pretending to read the late edition.

"This ain't a library, pal," the vendor says for the thousandth time today. "Buy it or book it."

I plop my change down and fold the paper up under my arm. I pull my collar up against the October breeze that likes to whip around the corners out of the alleyways, carrying all the trash that's hidden in the dark. The rain's let up, and the city smells like wet dog.

About a quarter after, I catch one of Marino's men skulking around outside Ice Pix, peeking in the window. He ducks down the alley to join his fellow garbage bags. The good thing about always being late is that everybody else is already there. The best thing about planning to be late is that you can watch them all show up.

After I headed home to my office this afternoon, I was met at the door by the Slipknot. He likes to show up unexpectedly and demand to run around town. The noose was still lying there in the chair. The mask was on the desk.

"I don't need you for this," I said out loud, and I swear I heard the husky whisper of his answer back.

"You can't do this without me."

"I can take care of Marino," I said.

"I mean life in general, Mann." His voice filled the room. "You can't do it without me."

That's the reason I still have a buzz on. I found the fifth in my drawer, and washed his voice outa' my head. I put on a nice red tie, the one with only a couple of stains, and left the noose in the chair. And I swear I left the mask on the desk. I know I did, but right now, as I reach for my piece under my coat, I feel something in my pocket. I pull the mask out and look through it.

I left it on the desk. I left it on the desk.

I shove it all back down inside and wipe the city grime from my eyes. It's dark now and I gotta go shed some light on the situation. I hand the paper back to the vendor.

"There a refund if there ain't no good news?"

19

"Good news'll cost you a lot more." The vendor looks at the paper. "I don't write it, I just peddle it."

I toss the rag down on his table and cross the street. I expect to be met by Marino's thugs, but I get to the door with no trouble. Something about this doesn't smell right.

"Your… visitors are over at the table." Bippy sweats. "They wouldn't go to the booth… considerin'… you know…"

"Table's fine, Bippy." I walk by.

"Look," he grabs my arm, "the bar's not full, but there may be folks you can't see. You get my drift?"

"I understand."

"I just don't want the place busted up," he says."Can you promise me that?"

"Did you have the other guys promise?" I pull my arm away.

Bippy starts taking bottles of the good stuff off the shelf and protects them under the counter.

The place is well lit tonight. That's usually a bad sign. Bippy's not usually one to show off the decor. The bar is sparse tonight. There's a few patrons at the stools and booths. Many of 'em are stealing looks at the man in the middle of the room.

Tentman is sitting at a large round table. His nurse is standing behind him like a statue, a bored statue, kinda' like one of those wooden Indians outside the butcher's shop on Cobble Circle.

"Your nurse can sit down," I say as I tip my hat to both of them.

"Her name is Mercy," Tentman has on these red glasses that obscure his eyes, "and she's my daughter."

"Well, she can sit." I sit. "She's attracting attention."

"She prefers to stand," he says.

"Suit yourself." I raise my hand to Bippy. "Drink?"

"I don't drink." Tentman's face doesn't seem to move beneath those wraps.

"Nothing?" I take off my hat. "No wonder you mummies are so dried out."

My attempt at humor doesn't seem so.

"Do you have my item?" He never moves, not even a pinky.

"You remember how hard it was raining the day you first came to my office?" I take the drink from Bippy. "I bet you got plenty wet that day."

"I paid a lot for this place," Bippy says in a whisper. "I'm still makin' payments. I don't wanna see it busted up."

"Now, this item you want…"

"I understood you already got it."

"You wanted me to steal it." I sip and look at him over the rim of the glass.

"Retrieve it," he says.

"Without any proof it was even yours."

"I assure you…"

Melanie comes out to the stage from the back. She's wearing the dress she had on earlier, but somehow it looks more alluring at night. It fits her like it was made to come off. She's going over the sheet music with her piano player while Tentman is busy assuring me. I call the ivory tickler Goose Egg

Henderson, which he thinks is because of his big goofy bald head, but it's mainly because he hates it.

"That was some day when you stopped by," I interrupt Tentman.

"Did you get it or not?" he asks. His daughter's grip tightens on his shoulders.

"You know, anybody could be under those wraps." I lean foreword and tap my finger on the thick oak table. "You're wanting me to say that I busted into the delivery ship holding goods that're heading to one of Veil City's top businessmen, and that I stole some precious ancient artifact from practically under his nose before he could even see it? Well, I can't honestly say that I'm the guy who did that."

"I remember the day I came to your office," he speaks deliberately.

"Oh, really?" I reach into my jacket where my Browning's perched.

"I just don't remember it being daytime," he says, "or raining, for that matter. The moon was full. I know that for certain, and there were possums in the trash can behind your building."

I take my hand out of my coat. "You can't be too careful."

"Yes… you can," he says. "You still have that coin I put down for the up-front payment?"

"The old pirate coin with the ship and eagle on it?" I raise an eyebrow. "Yeah, I haven't found a place that'll buy it yet. Everyone assumes it's hot. You and me know it's worth a heap, but everyone else is scared to go near it."

"It's not hot," Tentman says, "but I have an idea that might alleviate some apprehension."

"I don't think we're leaving here tonight without alleviating some tension." I look around.

"You have an idea?"

"I gotta little trick that might get things out in the open." I reach into my side pocket and pull out an old battered and folded envelope. I slide it across the table towards him.

"Here it is," I say in a voice loud enough to order a round. I take another drink to hide my poker face.

He doesn't move and neither does Mercy, but Melanie starts immediately singing her heart out.

"Do you mind telling me…" Tentman says.

"*Ba-da, BAA-da, boooo…*" Melanie purrs,

"*I like my man*
to understand
all my secrets and my…
satisfactions.
Beneath the veils,
I tell my tales with
all the twists and…
misdirections."

"Shhh," I put my finger to my lips, "I like this next part.

Two of Marino's men walk through the curtain in back and sit at the bar. Three more come in from the front door and pick a table by the exit.

"*So, show your dark…*
secrets, and I'll…
lift the veil and spark…

23

and you'll be my..."

"Jesus was betrayed for thirty pieces of silver," Tentman says over the music. "I hear these days you can get it for a song."

"...Mannnnn... doo-bee DWEEE, doo-bwah!"

I pull my spare black leather gloves out of my lower jacket pocket. I slide them down over my swollen fingers.

"Ssss..." I grit my teeth.

All the men get up on cue and head my way.

"Heya, Mann." The first tall broad shouldered man in the bright puke yellow tie sidles up to the table. "Whatcha' got goin' on? New friends?"

"Hey, Mustard," the other guy next to him in the black suit, white shirt and black and red tie says. "That *can't* be it."

"No, Bernie, it can't." Mustard looks up at Melanie, who quickly looks away and steps back over to the Goose Egg.

Bernie turns halfway around and whispers to Mustard, "That's, uh, Checkers, remember?"

I've noticed that since the Slipknot's been on the prowl, a lot of the nightlife has taken to giving itself nicknames. Mustard Plummer here is known for his yellow ties. Bernie Czeckelsby has been trying out Checkers.

"Hey, Mustard, Bernard... fella's." I nod as I place my hat on and tap it back into place.

"You sending a letter, Mann?" Mustard puts his hand down on the envelope.

"It's, uh, Checkers," Bernie adds under his breath. He leans forward a little. "I go by Checkers now. That's what all the guys are callin' me."

Mercy twitches until Tentman ever so lightly clears his throat.

"This the mailman?" Mustard smiles at Tentman.

"Tampering with the mail is a federal offense." I rub my chin.

"So, sue me." He turns it over in his hands.

He opens it up and takes out a worn note. "What's the meaning of this?" He tosses the scrap on the table in front of me. It has several large pound signs drawn on it.

"It's called, tic-tac-toe." I look at it. "I find that mysterious envelopes tend to draw people out."

Mustard lights up a smoke. He tosses the match on the floor and watches it burn out. Then he reaches down towards me. I tense to spring, but he doesn't attack. Instead, he flips my red tie to the side.

"Where's your new wardrobe, Mann?" He smiles and glances back at the men on both sides. "The Slipknot stayin' home this evening?"

"I don't need Slipknot to…"

"Maybe he don't wanna get shot no more," Bernie breaks in and laughs, "Hah!"

Mustard sneers and tosses his cigarette. He turns and grabs Bernie by the tie.

"Hup!" Bernie gasps.

"Go wait by the door, Bernie." Mustard gets in his face.

"Ch…Ch…Ch…" Bernie backs up.

Mustard gives him a shove. Bernie straightens his shirt and tie, clears his throat, and heads to the door.

"Okay, now…" Mustard turns back to me.

"Unlike some people," I say, "I don't need to hide behind a goofy prop tie to do my job."

Mustard slams his hands down and leans in on the table. The whole place listens. Everyone shuts it.

"Oh…" Melanie whimpers and tiptoes off stage behind the curtain.

"You ain't here for no tic-tac-toe," he says. "Cough it up, or me and the boys'll cough it up *for* ya'."

I feel the heat of the mask in my pocket.

"Don't kill them," Tentman says.

"I'm not going to kill them," I furrow my brow, "but I won't let…"

"I was talking to Mercy," he says.

She steps away from her father and right up next to Mustard. He points his thumb at her over his shoulder, and a big bruiser from in back of them steps up in between them. I take the opening to jump up and attack, but my face lands square into Mustard's oncoming fist.

"AH!" I fall backwards over my chair and land on the floor. Alla' the Beak's pounding from earlier comes back with Mustard.

Mercy kicks the big guy next to her, and he goes down on one knee. It was like she made his knee bend. Then she meets his face with her own knee. Blood spurts from his nose as his head flies back. Another guy tries to grab at her, and she keeps slapping his hands away, or slipping right through his fingers. Mind you, I'm seeing alla' this while Mustard and the other guys are tossing me back and forth like a medicine ball.

"Stop it!" Bippy yells. "Stop it now!"

An ice pick flies across the room, bounces on the table, and falls on the floor.

"That was supposed to…" He runs around the end of the bar and over to the table.

We all freeze and watch him as he picks up the pick and sticks it into the table.

"Yeah, I'll stop it all right now." Mustard pulls his piece out of his jacket holster.

All the customers that hadn't already headed for the door dive under their tables. A few of the women and a couple of the guys scream.

"Not in…" Bippy points at the door.

"Shut up!" Mustard points back, but with his gun.

Bippy shuts up.

"Cherry Picker, Sump Pump, grab the old man," Mustard directs. "We can stow him in the back of the truck."

"Those are really bad nicknames." I have my hands raised.

"No," Tentman says softly, "I can't let you do this."

"You ain't got no choice, old man." Mustard points the gun at him.

"Again, I was talking to Mercy." Tentman sighs. "Fine. Take me to Marino. It's not like I can fight back."

Mustard rotates back and forth with his gun pointed between me and Mercy. Bernie has his gun drawn too. Two men wheel Tentman out of the bar.

"You got two hours to get us the Golden Claw," Mustard says. "Too bad for the old man if you ain't got it, but something tells me you know where to look."

"This is stupid." I step towards him.

He holds the gun up at me. Mercy just glares at him and clenches her fists.

"Marino has got to know I don't…"

"Maybe you don't," Mustard starts backing to the door, "maybe it's the other guy that does."

"Other guy?"

"Tell him to pay us a visit, you know, in the place where he took the bullets," Mustard stands in the doorway. "Wear your tie, Mann! Have the Slipknot bring us the Golden Claw or this man dies."

"Should we call the cops?" Bippy asks after Mustard slams the door and leaves.

"You must be pretty desperate to think of the cops." I turn my chair back over and sit down. "You been drinking your own poison?"

Mercy pulls the ice pick from the table and flings it over the bar. It sticks like an arrow into the wall right between two bottles of whisky. She walks outa the place without saying a word.

"Not much of a conversationalist," Bippy says.

"Not much for making plans, either." I pull my hair back and put my hat on.

"What're you gonna do?"

"First things first," I say.

"Scotch?"

"Make it a double."

Chapter Four
Fighting Truth and Claw

There are some parts of the city where people still feel somewhat safe. Cops like to patrol the old Cobblestone Circle that used to be the town square years ago. Now it's a park. It's too dangerous for them to patrol other parts of town. Another crime free zone is around Marino's offices downtown. He owns one of Veil City's only skyscrapers, a brick and mortar and steel monstrosity that towers over its neighbors and casts a long shadow over the whole city.

Marino has a free pass. He owns this town. The law can't touch him while he can place hickeys all over the law. That doesn't stop the Slipknot from tightening around his neck, or at least it didn't. I found a trail of blood that led straight to Marino's schemes. He's a despot worse than any of the current crop over in Europe. While they're busy clawing for a bigger chunk of pie, Marino is content with his little cupcake kingdom. They might yet start a war, but Marino will profit from it.

"Nice tie." Mustard nodded. "Where's the mask?"

"I don't need the mask. You all know who I am."

I stand outside the doorway in the harsh streetlights outside the Zephyr Building. Mustard is taking up the entrance with his yellow tie and cigarettes. A couple of nondescript boxers file in behind him, dressed in gray suits and snub nosed boots.

"You mind if Pot Belly Kelly gives ya' a hug?"

One of the brutes steps up.

"Actually, I do." I step back and pull my jacket closed. "Nobody gets the claw before Marino. You think I'm carrying, you just plug me now. I betcha' he wants me alive and the claw unharmed."

"He don't give a tinker's darn about you, Mann," Mustard stops the thug, "but our orders were to bring you to the penthouse."

I step into the doorway and the three of them step aside. I stop in front of one of the thugs and poke him in the ribs.

"This man doesn't even have a pot belly," I say.

"It rhymes." Pot Belly Kelly smiles a gapped-tooth grin.

"Where's the girl?" Mustard sticks his head out the door.

"Don't know." I saunter into the foyer. "I wasn't told to bring a girl."

"You won't get a chance to pull no funny business." Mustard taps his jacket right over the gun he has resting beneath.

"No guns in the penthouse." I turn to him. "Remember?"

It hadn't been that long since Slipknot had it out with Marino. They fought it out in the penthouse of the Zephyr Building. Marino promised no guns. He had a bunch of eastern mojo he was wanting to test out, and some so called magic items that didn't do squat against the Slipknot. When Marino

finally got in a jam, the bullets came flying. Slipknot took one in the shoulder and one in the arm and one creased his hairline just above his ear.

He was still able to throw Marino through a plate glass window and down several floors through antique stained glass sky view ceilings.

I don't know how I got home, but all the doctoring was done to Slipknot by some private doc, and neither he nor Marino has been seen in public since then.

"I think he'll make an exception." Mustard lightly pushed on my shoulder in the direction of the elevators.

The elevator boy is an old man named Zorben Tindler. He's well known around town for doing odd jobs. Looks like tonight he's manning the old spring elevator. Me and Mustard and the boys get on, and the box drops about a foot.

"Hey, Zorben," I watch the gate close, "how's the wife and kids?"

"Still dead." The old man never even looks up. "You're supposed to ask me how's business."

"So how's this supposed to work?" I look over to Mustard.

"You hand over the claw, and Marino hands over the old man." Mustard sniffs and tightens his tie. "Easy, peasy."

The elevator stops for a second and the lights flicker. Everybody grabs a wall.

""Stupid relic!" Mustard composes himself. "This elevator musta' been built before the building was."

"So how's this really gonna work?" I straighten my hat.

"You hand over the claw, and me and the boys rough you up, take your gun and throw you through a plate glass window."

"Figured," I say. "And Tentman?"

"Guess the old man's one a' them old west heroes." Mustard pulls out a cigarette. "The boss'll probably set him up with some touring deal, if he'll play ball."

The elevator springs to a stop.

"Penthouse," Zorben announces, and we all step out like we're just out for a stroll.

Zorben closes the gate behind us.

"It has its ups and downs," he says. "Get it?"

Then he takes the elevator up to the roof instead of back down, revealing all the wires and cables beneath as the doors close.

The lights in the hallway are so bright, I can practically see through myself. They bump me down the corridor like I'm some sort of errant bowling ball.

"I know the way." I pull up and swing around. "I've been here before, see?"

Pot Belly goes for his gun, but Mustard slaps him in the shoulder.

"Stifle, ya' lunk," he says. "He's just gettin' jittery. He knows the score."

"What'll it take to buy you guys off?" I take a deep breath and start walking again. "A nice two bedroom house in the country with a white picket fence and a bulldog?"

"No dice." Mustard gives my shoulder a little extra shove. "We work for anybody else, we lose our life insurance."

"I like bulldogs." Pot Belly Kelly smiles.

The big oak double doors had been refinished since the last time. At a distance, they look like a million bucks. Up close, you can see the cracked veneer. Mustard swings them open like he's making some grand entrance, and the knotheads throw me into the dark room beyond.

It's like a cave in here. I wouldn't be surprised to see bats flying around. Last time it was all lit up like the hallway with fancy wall hangings and ornate furniture from the orient. This time, there's the big repaired plate glass windows in the back, letting in the soft neon blue of the city, and that's about it. Except way off in the front of the room, there's a desk and a light. There's a couple of guys sitting around the desk and as I get closer, they look like something out of a horror movie.

Mr. Tentman is still in his wooden wheelchair off to the side of the desk, just at the edge of the light from the desk lamp. Marino is sitting directly behind the desk. They're both colored by the light shining through the many hues of the Tiffany lampshade. Morino barely looks up.

He's packed in this full body cast thing. His neck is in a brace. One arm is in a cast with a sling over his shoulder. He's obviously wrapped up under his fancy suit. His face… his face looks like a jigsaw puzzle sewn together with a couple of pieces in the wrong spot. I can't tell if he is sneering or if he was just put back together that way. He's talking, but I can't hear him yet.

"Here you go, boss." Mustard pushes me up to the desk and pulls out his gun. "Say the word."

"No guns," Marino whispers and clears his throat. "No yet. Not unless I say so."

"You got it, boss." Mustard puts his gun back in his jacket, but keeps his hand on it.

"Mr. Tentman?" I look over.

"You brought it?" Tentman says.

"Heh, heh, heh, heh." Marino's voice grows clearer. "You see, the old man knows what's important."

I reach into my pants pocket. One of the thugs steps up outa' the darkness and grabs my arm. He sticks his hand down in my pocket with my hand.

"Buy me dinner first?" I scoff.

Pot Belly grabs the large gold coin and pulls it out of my pocket. He places it on the desk in front of Marino.

"So this is the fabled Golden Claw?" He turns the coin over in his good hand. "The one that brings good luck and health and stealth…"

"And wealth," I say, "like you need it."

"You can never have enough of any of those things," he smiles at me and Tentman, "especially the health part, right?"

"I'll just be taking Mr. Tentman and going." I walk over to the wheelchair and start pushing it across the large dark room.

"Yes, of course." Marino puts the coin in his outside top jacket pocket, "Except…"

"Oh, crap." I stop and roll my eyes.

"Except I already have two of these." He pulls a gun out from under the desk.

"I thought you said no guns." I step in front of Tentman, but the men at the exit draw their guns too.

"That was a stupid rule," Marino says. "I changed it to no guns for Runyan Mann."

"Oddly specific," I mumble.

Mustard walks up and sticks his hand in my coat like he knows me. He takes out my gun and sets it on the desk.

"The mask." Marino nods.

Mustard walks back over and plunges his hand back in.

"This coin is sixteenth century, I think." Marino looks past me to Tentman. "I read all about, *Alabaster Kid and the Pirate's Gold* by A. Severin. I thought it was pure fiction. Still, I sent my men out looking. I have a lot of men out looking for things. It's what I do."

"Wonderful." Tentman looks into the darkness. "With all that looking, you'd think they could see better."

Mustard takes my mask to Marino. It's like a part of me has left.

"I know what you mean." Marino holds my mask in his grubby hand. "I've been chasing after trinkets, and all along I had the most powerful artifact of them all."

"Slipknot's mask?" I take a step but am met with a gun in my ribs.

"How's it work?" Marino holds it under the light. "A magic word, a secret mechanism?"

"There's nothing... I mean, I don't know how..."

Mustard backhands me with the butt of his gun. I crumple like a house of cards that's just been smacked with the butt of a gun.

Marino puts the mask on.

"Oh, my." He starts to breathe faster. "I can feel it! It's working."

He creaks and pops and tries to stand up. He rises and takes the sling off his arm.

"Should we take him out?" Mustard points his gun down on me.

"Oh, no, Mr. Mustard." Marino starts walking. Each step breaks off splints and rods and wraps. "I'll take care of Mr. Mann myself!"

He looks like some kind of robot from the movies, like the tin man or something. I stand up and push Tentman into the darkness.

"Don't be ridiculous." I put up my fists. "There's nothing magical in that mask. It's all just to scare you mugs. I bought it at a costume shop."

"Then how do you explain *this*?" Marino swings high, and I duck. "How do you explain being able to take a gun full of bullets and still being able to pick up a full grown fighting man and throw him through a plate glass window?"

"Well, it's a mystery," I say. "You got me there."

"Yes," he sends a pile driver into my gut, "I sure did."

"ERK!" I slide across the floor on my posterior. That hurt worse than the dry heaves after New Year's.

I hear a scuffle behind me, and a gun goes off. They must miss me, because I'm still alive.

"Hold your fire!" Marino shouts. "I want him to myself!"

Nobody answers. They're too busy falling and being thrown into walls.

"The light, Mercy," Tentman says.

36

Someone's gun flies across the room and smashes the light cover. It knocks the light to the floor, but doesn't break the bulb. I take the opportunity to jump up and tackle Marino.

"Huhk!" We fall back towards the desk.

Mustard grabs my back but is pulled off by Tentman's silent daughter. He swings at her and misses. He points his gun. She slaps it aside and grabs his long yellow tie. He chokes and grabs at her hand as she pulls the knot tight. I stand to grab him, but my elbow is held by Marino. He throws me across the desk. As soon as I land, he's there, kicking me in the guts. I roll over and jump up. The pain still has me bent over but as he approaches, I land a solid punch to his face, right in the mask.

I gotta say… it felt good.

"Pfft!" Marino staggers back.

I walk up, but he recovers faster than I anticipate. He's on me in an instant, socking me in the head over and over. I'm getting punch drunk, when he stops hitting me and flies across the room. He can fly now?

There's a tall shadow where Marino just was. Tentman steps into the light, suddenly not looking so much the invalid.

"Sorry I waited." He walks right past me. "I thought you had it handled."

"I… I did have…" I lean on the desk.

At the count of about three punches and a couple of sickening cracks, Tentman hands Marino the floor. He drags him into the light and places the coin on the desk.

"Here," he says. "This is yours."

Mercy drops Mustard in an unconscious pile and hands me my gun. I stand up and put it back in the holster.

"How did…?"

"Now, I need the claw." Tentman places my mask on the desk.

"What are you going to do with Marino?"

"He's a wanted man." Tentman puts Marino into the wheelchair. "I'm taking him to jail. There's a federal bounty out on him."

"He'll just go free." I try to put the mask in my pocket, but my hand stops.

"Not a federal court," Tentman says.

Mercy is removing all the men's ties and using them to bind their hands behind their back.

"You don't understand," I say. "He's got people every-where. He'll just go free and get his record cleared."

"Not likely." Tentman starts to push him away.

"I can't let you take him." The Slipknot stands up straight and adjusts his mask. "There's only one judgement he can't escape."

"It's not for you to say." Tentman stops and pushes Mar-ino to Mercy.

She stands there and shakes her head at her father.

"Take him," he says.

Slipknot races over and places his hands on Mercy's shoulders.

"That's a mistake." Tentman tackles Slipknot, and they tumble into the darkness of the room.

Something breaks in Slipknot's face as rock hard fists pile in on him unerringly, like Tentman can see in the dark. The Slipknot feels nothing. In a jerking motion, he slips off to the side, causing Tentman to smack into the solid floor. He rises up in pain, and Slipknot puts his legs around Tentman's torso and squeezes. He pulls him foreword, smashing the old man's head into the wall. They both jump up. Slipknot can see Tentman's silhouette in the dim yellow light. It seems like his eyes are glowing. It gives Slipknot a target, as the two men stand there beating on each other. Blows become stronger rather than weaker. Each one shakes the other man through. Tentman lands a right hook to Slipknot's midsection, pulling all the air right out of him. Slipknot bends over, and Tentman lands on top of him. Instead of falling, though, Slipknot rises up and throws Tentman into the glass at the back of the room. Tentman gets to his feet, but is met by a charging Slipknot.

"RRRAAAHH!!" Slipknot slams him against the glass again and again until the glass cracks.

He grabs Tentman's head and beats a hole into the glass. Tentman brings his knee up and sends Slipknot staggering back. Both men try to catch their breath.

The yellow light swirls as Mercy comes down behind Slipknot with the lamp, and smashes it over his head. He goes down on his knees. She kicks him into her father, who beats into him with a left uppercut. They ping pong him back and forth until he lays unconscious on the floor.

I don't know what happens after that.

I hate hospitals. They're filled with sick people. Of course, sometimes they save lives. I'm not so sure I'd be waking up right now if I wasn't in one. Turns out, the same two people who were standing over Slipknot when he went down are standing over me when I wake up. I try to move, but nothing listens.

"Don't move," Tentman says, and my body listens to him. "You're in no shape to move around."

I moan and look down at myself. I'm nearly as wrapped up as Tentman is.

"How can you…?"

"I heal well," he says.

"Obviously." I sink down into the pillow. "You get your claw?"

"It was around your neck the whole time." Tentman pulls a necklace out of his shirt around his neck.

"Alla' this for a shriveled up old bird claw." I give one small laugh. It's all I can muster. "And it ain't even gold."

"Belief is a powerful thing." Tentman looks up at Mercy who heads for the door.

"Is belief in the claw how you can walk?"

"No." He pulls a hospital wheelchair around to the side of the bed. "That was just a lie to get me close to Marino."

"You don't understand how powerful he is," I say.

"You're right." Tentman takes out his gun. "We have to get you out of here. Marino has at least a dozen men in this building heading this way to take you out."

"I'll never make it." I can barely move. "I can barely move."

"We'll find a way."

"My mask," I say. "*His* mask, do you have it?"

"It won't matter." Tentman goes to the door. "You have multiple broken bones…"

Mercy throws my mask onto my chest.

"*You* put it on," she says, "and *you* be responsible for it."

I grit my teeth and slowly pick my mask up in my broken hands.

"Get him in the chair," Tentman says. "They're heading this way."

I drop the mask onto the rags around my bloodied eyes. It seems to snap down and push the gauze aside. I sit up. I'm wrapped in cloth from head to foot. I turn in the bed and simply stand up. I slip my pants and jacket on like it's Sunday morning.

"Good luck." Mercy tightens the noose around my neck and places the Golden Claw over the top of it.

"Thanks," I walk out the door past them, "but I'm not the one who's gonna need it."

End

Flip the book over to read

THE Alabaster Kid
BENEATH THE VEIL

FLIP THE BOOK OVER TO READ

and the Golden Claw